T0245888

FLIGHTLESS
FALCON

FLIGHTLESS
FALCON

James Charles Smith

BROWN BOOKS
PUBLISHING GROUP

Flightless Falcon

Brown Books Publishing Group
Dallas, TX/New York, NY
www.BrownBooks.com
(972) 381-0009

A New Era in Publishing®

Publisher's Cataloging-In-Publication Data

Names: Smith, James Charles, 1950- author.
Title: Flightless falcon / James Charles Smith.
Description: Dallas, TX ; New York, NY : Brown Books Publishing Group, [2024]
Identifiers: ISBN: 9781612546674 (paperback) | 9781612546681 (ebook)
Subjects: LCSH: Hitchhiking--United States--Fiction. | Young men--United States--History--20th century--Fiction. | Conscientious objection--Fiction. | Vietnam War, 1961-1975--Public opinion--Fiction. | United States Air Force Academy--Students--Fiction. | United States-- History--1961-1969--Fiction. | LCGFT: Historical fiction. | Road fiction. | BISAC: FICTION / Coming of Age. | FICTION / Historical / 20th Century / Post-World War II. | FICTION / Biographical.
Classification: LCC: PS3619.M58831 F55 2024 | DDC: 813/.6--dc23

ISBN 978-1-61254-667-4
LCCN 2023947469

Printed in the United States
10 9 8 7 6 5 4 3 2 1

For more information or to contact the author, please go to www.AuthorJamesCSmith.com.

Flightless Falcon is dedicated to my family, who have encouraged me throughout this process, buoying my spirits when I had doubts. Particularly, it is dedicated to my late wife, Brenda Cashion Smith. Although she passed before she could read my efforts, she lives on in the better attributes of the women I attempted to portray in these pages.

The estimates of deaths and injuries due to the Vietnam War vary widely. Considering US forces only, there were approximately 58,000 US servicemen killed and 153,000 wounded (and 150,000 more that did not require hospitalization). Estimates of total deaths by all parties in Vietnam, Cambodia, and Laos during twenty years of fighting range from 1.5 million to 3.6 million.

1 ———————————————— April 26, 1969

Sam Roberts shuffled back and forth, stomping his feet to get his blood flowing. Light, cold gusts of wind whispered across the plains on the outskirts of Lafayette, Colorado, about twenty-five miles east of Boulder. He saw that the ground was bare, and the dirt was sprinkled with short, softly rustling, brown grass. Stunted trees sought protection from the wind in creek gullies and other shallow depressions. A distant tractor chugged, but he could hear no traffic on the road. A few cows stood in an adjacent field, facing away from the wind. One of them raised her head and lowed at Sam.

He faced west toward the late afternoon sunset. The distant Rocky Mountains were mere diminished bumps on the horizon. Just beyond them, he observed heavy black clouds, approaching and growing higher each time he looked, soon obscuring the summits. A late-April snowstorm had been forecasted. He could smell the icy moisture in the air, combined with a faint scent of cow manure and dirt. The wind rose, and he zipped up his wool coat against the cold.

He had been standing for hours on the side of Colorado Route 7, hoping for a ride east. Long periods with no cars partially accounted for his extended wait, but he also suspected that some motorists were wary about picking up a lone six-foot-tall man. He had just resigned from the United States Air Force Academy and was hitchhiking home to St. Louis, about a thousand miles away. Sam had hitchhiked before, but never over such a distance.

The air force had given him an airline ticket to fly back to St. Louis. Being practically broke, he had wanted the $120 in his pocket instead. A kind lady with a gentle smile at the airport ticket counter was very helpful and helped him get exactly that by exchanging the ticket for cash. Maybe the extra money would provide a buffer to his current uneasiness.

He was dressed in jeans and an Air Force Academy Falcons sweatshirt. The only official Air Force Academy clothing he wore was a hooded wool peacoat with USAFA stitched on the breast. It was air force blue and was the only coat he owned. He wore his black combat boots, which were issued when he first arrived for basic training last June. His B4 duffel bag was stuffed full and nearly as large as him. It sat beside him on the roadside. Except for his short, stubby haircut, he thought he almost looked like a normal civilian, or maybe an escaped monk. He rummaged through his bag and found a ski cap.

Sam's girlfriend, Cheryl, had dropped him on the roadside hours ago. They had discussed her driving him all the way home, but as much as they wanted to stay together as long as possible, it was at least a two-day drive there and back. And that was if she drove like a maniac. She could afford neither the expenses nor the time. Saving money was the reason he was having to hitchhike in the first place, so he was useless.

Since resigning, he had been staying with Cheryl in her house in Boulder. What a dreamlike stay it was. They had hardly left her house the whole time. They had worn each other out. Sam closed his eyes and relived the feeling of their bodies together and the comfort of her company.

He thought of their time together as a peaceful bridge between a stressful past and a murky future. Both of them wanted him to stay, but they knew that their lives would not allow that, at least for now. Instead, Sam watched her drive away. What awaited him after a hitchhike back home would be an uncertain existence and certain parental disapproval.

A blue Chevrolet truck approached from the west. It started slowing down about a hundred feet from him. Sam felt great relief and picked up his bag. He could see an older man peering out the windshield at him. But when the truck rolled alongside him, the driver looked straight ahead and instead hit the gas pedal. The truck sped past, its engine roaring.

Sam dropped his bag and kicked a pebble off the shoulder of the road. It was getting colder. He ached for Cheryl's warm touch and soft manner. He buttoned his coat around his throat and tried to empty his mind.

It had been several months earlier, in February, when Sam had finally decided he would resign from the Air Force Academy. He had been stewing over his situation since he first arrived for training at the academy in June of 1968. He immediately felt deep in his gut that it was wrong for him. Though he could not rationally explain why, he continually felt an out-of-body experience of being in the wrong place at the wrong time. He did not like the person he was becoming because of the academy's training. Cadet life was filled with hassle and stress. He could not picture a goal worthy of enduring that. As time passed, he was also becoming more disillusioned about a military career in general and about the Vietnam War in particular.

The slow, grinding process of reaching a decision from the conflicting thoughts and events swirling in his head had been debilitating. Each path seemed to have its own advantages but also its own dire consequences. Lately, he had felt weak and anxious as he struggled to make up his mind. His body ached, and he felt sick much of the time. He could not recall when he last felt unconditionally happy. Having finally decided on a course of action, excitement and awe over his approaching freedom were added to this toxic brew of jumbled feelings. It was a perplexing mix.

On the day he chose to resign, he postponed his actions until after dinner. He needed to will himself to get out of his chair and execute the choice he had made. He stood up and walked out of his dorm room. When indoors, grunts had to walk at attention almost everywhere they went. When outdoors, they had to run at attention. This was an ungainly process of walking or running with their heads and necks still and their arms moving stiffly by their sides. Anytime a grunt passed an upperclassman anywhere outside the classroom buildings, he had to stop in place, swivel like a toy soldier to face the cadet, and yell at the top of his voice, "Good afternoon, sir!"—or whatever part of the day it was. Now travelling down the hall, even at attention, his gait was unsteady. His shaky legs did not fully control the placement of his feet. He sweated as if he had a fever, despite the reasonable temperature in the dorm. His head was smoldering, and he could feel his heart racing.

He stumbled up to the dorm room door of Cadet Captain Winston: a first classman who was also Sam's flight leader and immediate supervisor. Policy dictated that Sam go through his chain of command with matters like this. He hesitated outside Winston's door, even once turning to leave and then changing his mind. Finally, he knocked.

"Come in," said a voice inside.

Sam resisted the urge to run away. He could feel his face flush, but he opened the door. Winston's room was clean and spartan with two single beds on opposite sides, each with a bedstand, dresser, and desk—like every other cadet's room. Winston and his roommate did not need to meet the absurd grunt cleanliness standards, but the room was still reasonably orderly. At least they had a stereo.

Winston sat at his desk reading a textbook. He looked up at Sam, a little irritated at the interruption.

Sam entered the room, snapped to attention and shouted, "Good evening, sir," as was required for fourth classmen addressing their superiors.

"At ease," said Winston. "What can I do for you, Cadet Roberts?"

Sam's body relaxed only slightly. He started to answer, but his words came out as a croak. He stopped and cleared his throat. "Excuse me, Cadet Captain Winston, sir," he said, his voice wavering. "I wish to state my intention to resign from the US Air Force Academy."

Winston looked up with concern in his eyes. "What's going on?" He paused. "Are you sure?"

"Yes, sir, I am sure."

"OK, and what's your reason?"

Sam had rehearsed his answer to be crisp and to the point. Now he could not remember what he had practiced. "I no longer want to be a career officer in the air force," he blurted out. "This life is just not cut out for me, sir."

Winston scowled and said, "There's got to be more to it than that."

Sam squirmed. "Well, I also have problems with the Vietnam War. I don't feel it's right, and I definitely don't want to participate fighting in it, sir."

"OK," said Winston. "You think you're the only one here who thinks that way?"

Sam was not expecting that answer. He felt his determination erode slightly. "I suppose not," he said, "but how can I stay in the air force with those doubts?"

"I don't think anyone who serves in the military totally agrees with every assignment or mission he or she gets," Winston said carefully. "We also can't always choose exactly how that mission is accomplished. The bottom line is that we all serve and protect our country. That is our real mission and duty. Look around. You couldn't find a better group of men to share that mission with."

Sam thought about Winston's words, considering whether he needed to reveal his more personal reasons. He decided this was neither the place nor time. "I hear what you're saying, and you state it very well. But I'm sorry, sir. That's just not enough for me."

Winston shook his head. "Personally, I wish you would stick around. You have done well here. Any way I can talk you out of it?"

"I appreciate that, sir. You've done a great job trying to. But I've made up my mind."

Winston paused and tapped his index finger on his desk. "Well, that's too bad." He then stated more formally, "If that's the case, that is your right. Your intention is noted and will be passed on, Cadet Roberts."

Sam shifted his feet as Winston continued to stare at him. He looked away.

"We'll start the process," said Winston. "Is that all?"

Sam had nothing left to say. "Yes, sir, that's all," he finally answered.

"Then you are dismissed."

Sam started to turn away, but then looked back at Winston. "Sir, I assume you don't mean I am dismissed from the academy."

Winston turned his attention back to his book, hiding his smile. "Not yet, smart ass. Now go away."

Sam smartly executed an about-face and marched like a toy soldier to the door. Out in the hall, he saw no one else around. He was still shaking but also felt the tension starting to melt. He smiled as he walked about twenty feet down the hall, control of his feet returning. He couldn't help but dance sideways as he did so.

A cadet was usually allowed to leave about two weeks after resigning. But six weeks later in April, Sam and his roommate, Derek, were still sitting at their desks in their austere dorm room. Derek had also quit in February. He was older than Sam, having previously served as an enlisted man in the regular air force. At the end of the school year in May, cadets were promoted to the next class. Only a few months remained until they would become third classmen and could act relatively human. They still looked like normal cadets at this point. They still wore their uniforms: dark blue pants and a light blue oxford shirt with black-and-silver shoulder boards that showed rank. Theirs showed only one silver line, meaning they could not be ranked any lower.

They had been only partly engaged in cadet life for the past weeks. They were directed to eat separately with a few other malcontents and washouts, lest they "contaminate" the good ones. They were not going to complete the spring semester, so they stopped going to classes. They could go around the campus, but there was not much to do, and they avoided direct confrontations with other cadets if they could.

Sam was reading a book at his desk. He put the book down and turned to Derek. "Any news?" asked Sam.

"Nope," answered Derek. "The papers are still sitting on the superintendent's desk."

Although no one openly said so, Sam suspected his own academic ranking was high enough that the academy wanted to keep him. Derek was president of the freshman class, so Sam could see why the air force wanted him to stay. Whatever the reasons, both had been subjected to weeks of Good Cop/Bad Cop treatment tailored to reconvince them to do their duty.

One "good cop" general had sat at the other end of a long conference table and told him, "We understand that the Air Force Academy needs to change. We need leaders like you to help us change it." Sam was inspired and almost convinced, until he tried to envision the general consulting with him at the same huge table about grave academy matters. *Right, like that would happen.*

That meeting was followed almost immediately by a "bad cop" colonel who resorted to, "Don't you think you owe your country anything, son? Do you think our freedoms have no cost?" This didn't have the effect they wanted it to have.

2 ———————————— March 15, 1969

A fourth classman (still called a grunt) stood at attention in the dormitory hallway under a clock, shouting out the time, weather, and other announcements. His voice reverberated off the hard walls and floor. Other cadets were in the hallway, grunts walking stiffly at attention and turning square corners, while the upperclassmen walked normally. Some were dressed; others headed for the showers.

In their room, Derek had had enough. He put his hands firmly on his desk and told Sam, "No more of this bullshit!"

There and then, they pledged to no longer participate in the underclass games. They were still sharply dressed in their uniforms, showing their class and rank, but instead of running around at attention, they sauntered about, walking casually, raising their hands to upperclassmen and mumbling, "Hey man," or, "How's it hanging?"

Both wondered why they had waited so long. They had unearthed a remarkable fact: small mistakes caused aggressive behavior from the upperclassmen. Slightly scratched dress shoes, a missed trivia question, a misplaced glance—all caused the upperclassmen to bristle up and attack. But Sam's and Derek's totally outrageous acts, following no rules whatsoever, brought a different response. The upperclassmen became uncomfortable and avoided them altogether. Any upperclassman who saw one of them approaching would lower his eyes and try to turn away.

Back in their room, Sam turned to Derek.

"It's incredible. They get really flustered."

"It's like we're the crazy Indians in the Sioux tribes," Derek said. "The normal Sioux held them in awe."

Just then, an upperclassman walked through their door. His uniform shoulder boards showed he was a third classman, or sophomore. Sophomores were usually the most vicious. Only recently absolved from receiving torment, they were now the most eager to give it. This third classman was unfamiliar to them.

Sam and Derek sat with their feet on their desks, facing the door.

The upperclassman bellowed and spat, "You worthless grunts. Don't you know you're supposed to snap to attention when an upperclassman enters your room?"

In a low, menacing voice, Derek said, "Get your ass out of our room before we kill you."

The cadet froze, and his mouth dropped open. He glanced right and left to see if anyone else had heard. Seeing no one, he slowly backed out of the room and rushed away. Sam and Derek looked at each other.

"Point taken," said Sam. They both laughed.

Finally, on the morning of April 23, after weeks of self-doubt over whether he was making the right choices and worrying about his fate because of them, Sam phoned the superintendent's staff sergeant to check his status. He couldn't think of anything else he could do.

"I think we are about to process your request," the sergeant told him. "But you may have to walk off your tours before we let you go."

A tour was a punishment where you marched alone outside for an hour, in full parade regalia with an M1 rifle on your shoulder. Sam thought, with all the demerits he had accumulated through his "Holy Sioux" phase, he would be marching tours until he was thirty. "I think I'll call my congressman," was all Sam said.

Those turned out to be the magic words.

"Call back in fifteen minutes," the sergeant replied before hanging up.

Sam circled the pay phone like a caged panther. He tried to take a walk but kept gravitating back to the phone. After exactly fifteen minutes, he made the call.

"You are approved to begin processing out," the sergeant stated.

Sam's knees buckled, and he almost fell. "Thank you, thank you, thank you!" blurted Sam into the phone. He left the phone dangling off the hook and danced down the hallway, jumping into the air to click his heels.

He stopped and ran back to the phone, frantically searching his pockets for change. He fed the phone and called Cheryl. "Honey, I'm out!" he shouted as soon as he heard her pick up.

"You're out now?" she shouted back.

"Well, no, but they've started the process. I may get out later today. I expect them to throw me out the door anytime now."

"Oh baby," she said through her tears. "Finally! Oh my God, you just get yourself up here to me."

"I will as soon as I can. Tonight, if I can, but in the morning if I can't."

"I'll be here. I love you."

"I love you too," said Sam as he hung up the phone.

Sam walked through the academy gate merely two hours after that. All of his paperwork had been neatly organized, and he had signed where he was told. It was all business. Sam suspected that the academy was eager for him to leave too.

Now Sam was jumping into an undefined void, feeling eager and anxious at the same time.

An air force staff sergeant drove him out the gate, en route to the Colorado Springs Airport, in the late afternoon to put him on a plane to St. Louis. The sergeant ignored him the entire time. He was making it clear that he knew Sam was resigning and that he did not feel warm and friendly about it.

During the long, silent ride, the sergeant behaved like Sam was carrying some infectious disease, or as if he would have been driven mad if they actually talked. At least such talk could potentially make the sergeant less military minded if he was able to see Sam's side of things. But instead the sergeant stared straight ahead and gripped the wheel tightly as he drove, refusing to even give Sam the time of day.

He stared out the window. Sam had become familiar with such attitudes over the last six weeks waiting for his release, and he was not going to let those attitudes, or the sergeant, ruin this big moment. He was free, dammit. Despite his resolve, his face flushed in anger at the sergeant's disapproval, and he experienced a flash of shame at the idea that he had gotten it wrong and was letting people down.

The sergeant pulled up to the terminal and stopped at the departures gate. Sam opened his door and stepped to the curb. After the sergeant slowly opened his door and walked to the back of the car, he opened the trunk, grabbed Sam's bag, and tossed it onto the sidewalk like a gigantic bag of dirty diapers. He got back in the car without a word and drove away.

Without much conviction, Sam raised his right hand with his middle finger extended and muttered, "And good fucking luck to you too, sergeant."

3 ——————————————— April 23, 1969

After Sam dragged his bag to the ticket counter and received his $120 refund, he found a pay phone to call his parents to tell them he was released.

Sam's dad, L.D., was a captain and pilot in the US Army Air Corps when he first met Sam's mom, Sarah, in Grand Island, Nebraska, during World War II. She worked at the Officer's Club at the airfield. His B-29 squadron was based there, and they were preparing to fly the planes to Tinian Island in the Pacific. From there, the bombers could reach mainland Japan. They were married shortly before L.D. took off. L.D. flew twenty-five missions from Tinian Island to the Japanese mainland during the most terrifying war in world history. L.D. and Sarah continued to build a family when he returned. Included in it were Sam's two older sisters, Jill and Kay.

Sam deposited a quarter into the payphone and dialed his parents' number. His dad answered the phone.

"I just got released," said Sam. "I'll be heading home soon."

"Do you have *any* idea what you're going to do next?" his dad asked.

"I'll get a job until I can get back in school," Sam answered.

"I wish I could understand what you're doing, son. Why do you insist on throwing away this great opportunity? Don't you know what an honor it is to be chosen for any of the service academies? But here you go again, making a rash decision."

Sam blew his breath out in frustration. His voice grew louder. "I've been thinking about this for almost a year now, so it's far from a quick decision I just came up with yesterday."

"When did you get so damn antimilitary? The air force has provided a good life for all of us, dammit."

Sam was not close to his father, but he respected his service and courage. Sam had actually enjoyed being an air force brat, so he did not consider himself to be antimilitary at all. In fact, he was proud to be associated with the military and considered it to be an honorable profession—just not the profession for him.

"Who said I'm antimilitary?" Sam yelled. He could hear his mom crying in the background.

"It makes no sense," his dad said. "I just don't understand."

"You certainly won't understand me as long as you keep shouting at me and not listening. It's just not what I want to do with my life. Maybe I can do something else you might be proud of."

His father became angrier. "Why do you have to be so pigheaded?"

Sam heard his mom in the background say, "Where do you imagine he got that?"

His dad then yelled at his mom. "You putting this on me? This is my fault?"

"Settle down, L.D. It's no one's fault," she answered.

But his dad was undeterred. "It's time you learn that sometimes you must do what you need to do, not always what you want to do. You just need to do your duty like I and many others have done."

The thing was Sam felt that he *needed*, not wanted, to leave the Air Force Academy, but it was clear he could not convince his father of this. When they hung up, nothing had been resolved.

His dad was a colonel when he retired from the air force into civilian life a few years ago. He had signed up for the "My Country, Right or Wrong" mentality and now was worried about what he considered to be the two greatest threats to civilization: rust and communism. Sam had expected his dad to oppose his actions, but he was still hurt by the lack of support and surprised by his vehemence. His mother was softer in her response but still followed his dad's lead.

Standing before the pay phone at the airport and wishing for a happier phone call, Sam tried to call Cheryl. But there was no answer.

He wrestled the bag back outside to the arrival gate and scouted his next move. He yearned to get to Cheryl, but he thought it was too late in the day to start hitchhiking to Boulder. The air force had given Sam a small travel allowance. He would use that to stay in Colorado Springs. He surveyed his surroundings. He saw a Ramada Inn across the airport parking lot. He looked over all the cars and buses near the gate and saw that right in front of him at the curb was the Ramada Inn shuttle bus. Sam smiled and said to himself, "Looks like a sign to me."

He checked in at the front desk and paid cash. After that, he pushed and pulled his bag down the long hallway to his room, the florescent lights flickering as lazy orchestral music played on the motel's sound system.

He opened the door to his room and dropped his bag on the floor. He felt as light as a gazelle without the bag tying him to one spot like a ball and chain. When he walked over to the window and opened it, a rush of fresh, cool air brushed his face. The smell of the pine trees, but also a slight hint of jet fuel, auto exhaust, and cheap restaurant food hit him. Sam thought it smelled of adventure.

From his window, he saw a large white building about a half-mile away in the dusk. A large red *K* shown like a beacon from the building.

"Ahh, K-Mart," he sighed appreciatively.

He had not been in a store for a long time. There were not many retail opportunities at the Air Force Academy, so K-Mart seemed like a shopping paradise. Because of these limited retail opportunities, unless his parents sent something in a care package, he wasn't getting squat. The academy commissary was as forbidden to Sam and his grunt classmates as the sacred recesses of the High Temple of Karnak. He reveled at the thought of no more such restrictions in his life. No one was there to tell him what to do or how to do it. His skin tingled in anticipation. He opened the door and rushed through it, slamming the door on his way out

As he walked into the K-Mart, he squinted under the harsh white light flooding the store's cavernous space. The isles seemed to stretch to a distant horizon. The shelves were crowded with all manner of merchandise, from food and clothing to tools and hardware. He smelled a mix of plastic packaging and the sharp aroma of industrial-grade disinfectant cleaner. Bland music played over the public-address system. He was overwhelmed by the limitless selection.

He spent more than an hour roaming the store but was limited to what he could stuff in his duffel bag back in his room. He bought a sleeping bag made from "the latest synthetic materials," and he thought it was relatively light, warm, and compact. Well worth the $14.96 he paid for it. Even more worth it was when Sam felt more self-reliant now that he owned it. He also bought a foldable shovel/trenching tool, a can of spinach, a jar of peanut butter, and a loaf of bread, which completed his groceries. At the checkout, he threw in a newspaper, the *Colorado Springs Gazette-Telegraph*.

He walked back to the Ramada Inn with his stuff. He used the can opener blade on his pocketknife to open the can of spinach. He ate it right out of the can, just the way he had when he was a kid. He had always loved the stuff. It worked well if you were unable, or too lazy, to cook. Then he took a spoon from a small container of camping supplies in his bag and made a peanut butter sandwich.

"See, Mom, I have a balanced diet," he said, pointing proudly to it.

It was early in the evening, and Sam was looking forward to going out on his first free night. He was also hungry for good times. But he also knew he needed to make his ticket money last. He did not know when he would get more. Whatever he did had to be cheap. He opened the newspaper to the entertainment section and read as he munched on his sandwich.

The Ice Capades were performing at the Denver Coliseum. Tickets were $1.50.

"Too wholesome," he said with his mouth full of peanut butter. Besides, it was in Denver.

The Lion in Winter with Peter O'Toole and Katherine Hepburn was held over for the fourth week at the Cinema 70 for $2.00.

"Too snooty," he said.

The Sky Vue Drive-In had a Clint Eastwood double feature with *Fistful of Dollars* and *A Few Dollars More* for $1.25. Kids were free.

"That's more like it," he said. Sam paused for a moment and snapped his fingers. "Damn! No car, no drive-in."

As a fourth classman, Sam had been living in a cultural desert and news blackout for almost a year. Fourth classmen could not own radios, and TVs were as rare as grand pianos on academy grounds. The newspaper he had bought was his first glimpse into the wide world after a long time. He opened and scanned the front page to see what he could find out. And find out he did.

North Vietnam battalions were moving back from threatening Saigon but appeared to be preparing for another offensive.

Chancellor Maurice B. Milton of the University of Denver labeled Cornell, Columbia, and Harvard national disgraces as a result of student disturbances tolerated there.

Sirhan B. Sirhan was sentenced to death for the assassination of Senator Robert F. Kennedy, but appeals to higher courts could spare him indefinitely.

Black students at Cornell were protesting the university's disciplinary actions against five other black students. Some of the students brandished firearms.

Police charged a rioting Irish mob in Belfast. The rioters met the police with a hail of rocks, chunks of steel, and firebombs.

Sam didn't want to dwell on those stories his first day out. He knew there was no shortage of conflict—not in the US or elsewhere in the world. And he couldn't help but wonder if peace would ever be possible, or if humans were predestined to aggression since the throwing of rocks at each other across campfires.

As a young teen, he had been exposed to many things such as the Cuban Missile Crisis, the assassination of John F. Kennedy, and the racial injustice and strife of the sixties. Sam could even vividly remember the duck-and-cover drills at school where they had huddled under their desks in the illogical belief that it would protect them in the case of a nuclear attack. That was about the time that backyard bomb shelters started to appear in suburban neighborhoods.

He had grown up bracing for the fiery death that faced him and would be only minutes away if the Russians decided to launch their missiles. Over time, the Cold War and the overhanging nuclear threat simply became the status quo. But during the Cuban Missile Crisis, everyone was tethered to their radios and TVs, waiting for word of shots being fired between Russian and US warships, causing the world to be sucked into nuclear destruction. People soon even adapted to cope with their fear, pushing it back into their minds, which eventually dulled and reduced itself to a background dread. These familiar threats were still in Sam's mind but were far overshadowed by the Vietnam War and the draft. That aspect was personal to him and impossible to ignore.

Seeking lighter thoughts, Sam turned to the sports section and found the baseball standings. He saw the Chicago Cubs were in first place in the Eastern Division of the National League.

"Like that will last," said Sam to himself. His Cardinals were within reach, and the season had just started.

Wilt Chamberlain's Lakers were playing Bill Russell's Celtics in the first game of the NBA finals. Sam felt Chamberlain and Russell were the two best centers in basketball, maybe in history. The two giants seemed to rise to new heights when facing each other.

Sam read an advertisement in the back of the sports section, which hawked an American Motors Rambler featuring room for six adults and a peppy 128 horsepower engine, listed for $1,999.

"Guess I'll keep hitchhiking for a while," Sam said. He could not imagine himself getting $1,999 together any time soon.

Sam was eager to go out on the town. He remembered it was legal in Colorado to drink a 3.2 percent beer at the age of eighteen. On his last night before reporting to the academy in 1968, he had gone to a bar and gotten to see Mitch Ryder and the Detroit Wheels. It was a good way to end his freedom. Now some great rock 'n' roll, a few beers, and some spirited companions were even better ways to start his freedom once again.

First, he would just rest a minute on the bed and watch TV. When he turned it on, Fess Parker filled the small screen in Daniel Boone's coonskin cap, carrying his long flintlock rifle.

Sam didn't even remember closing his eyes.

When he woke before dawn, he checked out of the Ramada Inn and started his hitchhike from Colorado Springs to Boulder. So much for the better ways to start his freedom.

His senses soon became sharpened by his unfamiliar surroundings, his sight and hearing seemingly more vivid. The mountains behind Colorado Springs glowed in the rising sun, the crisp red rock partially covered with rich green pines. He smelled the pines even above the highway scents of oil and gasoline, and he could taste what he smelled in the back of his mouth. The traffic on I-25 was still light, but the rush and roar of passing cars and the background drone of all the traffic was enveloping. All was new.

4 ——————————— September 1968

Cheryl and Sam had met during their senior year in high school. He was attracted to her the first time he met her, but she was dating Ted, one of Sam's acquaintances. He felt obligated by the "dating code" to simply cool his jets and be just a good friend to Cheryl. As friends, they talked and confided with each other about things they hadn't been able to with anyone else. She revealed the reasons for some unexplainable—at least to him—female behavior. Sam, in return, attempted to explain why men acted like bozos a good bit of the time.

When he discovered that Cheryl was going to the University of Colorado, he contacted one of her old friends for her address. He wrote her a letter. She wrote back, telling him that she and Ted had broken up. That fact completely altered his intentions of reviving their friendship; he decided to pursue something more instead. She included her phone number and encouraged him to call her. It certainly didn't take much convincing.

He gathered all the change he could find and went to a pay phone. It was a relatively private phone and free from upperclassmen harassment. He tried to steady his trembling hands as he fed the coins into the pay phone. He dialed Cheryl's number. When she answered, the sound of her voice caused him to shiver.

"Hello, Cheryl. This is Sam."

"Oh, Sam, I'm so glad you called me. I hope you didn't call a bunch before someone answered. We're not here much."

"No, lucky me. This was my first try. It's so great to hear your voice."

"Oh, it's so wonderful to hear yours. I've missed you."

His initial apprehension began to dissolve, and they immediately returned to their familiarity with one another. They talked for a long time while he kept feeding change into the phone. The words seemed to flow effortlessly between them. He decided to take a leap.

He stammered, "Uh . . . you know I was always very attracted to you in high school."

She paused for a moment. "Well duh!" she giggled. "You think I didn't know that? You were also too befuddled to see that I was attracted to you too."

They were off to the races. Sam felt a thrill knowing the love stemming from their friendship could potentially evolve into something more. He could imagine himself touching her, kissing her. Better yet, Cheryl touching and kissing him back. Those thoughts made him feel warm inside.

They agreed to meet up at the Air Force Academy versus University of Colorado football game in October. He would have a day pass but would have to return to the academy on a bus later that night. Only seniors, or first classmen, were allowed to own cars.

When the AFA buses arrived for the football game, they pulled into a parking lot reserved for them. Through the bus's open window, he saw and heard pennants flapping on top of the coliseum. It was sunny, and the autumn day saw to it that the leaves had started to turn colors. A noisy crowd filled the parking lot between the buses while diesel exhaust filled the air. He heard band music inside the stadium and smelled fried food from the concession stands. As he stepped down to the pavement, he saw Cheryl waiting in the parking lot. He recognized her auburn hair blowing in the wind.

They had talked over the phone but had not seen each other in five months. He couldn't believe they had grown so close and not laid eyes on each other for so long. He fretted about what she would think of his hair, or the lack of it. He had recently been required to get a haircut, so there was only a little fuzz at the top. His hair had been much longer in high school.

She was dressed in Colorado's colors, sporting a short black skirt; a gold long-sleeved T-shirt; and high, black leather boots. Sam's breath caught. He could not believe his good fortune in having someone so stunningly beautiful in his life.

She was tall and lean, full-figured and athletic. Her fine, straight nose was slightly freckled, as were her high cheek bones. Her hazel eyes sparkled with happiness at seeing him again. Sam loved her lips—full, but with a slight permanent pucker. She smiled as she brushed her long straight hair from her face. This certainly softened the knot of tension within him, and all uncertainty suddenly vanished.

"Hey," she said, pointing at her outfit. "Be true to your school! Right?"

"Damn right," he answered, pointing to his uniform. "Sportin' a little blue here myself."

She beamed, ran into his arms, and wrapped her own around him. Besides a few platonic kisses on the cheek, they had never kissed before. When he leaned into her face, the bill of his uniform hat poked her in the forehead. He had to break the hug to remove it. They laughed at their awkwardness and came together again. Her lips were soft, and he tasted her lipstick. He saw her eyes flit up to his hair. She smiled and stroked what was left of it, softly brushing the fuzz with her fingertips.

"I don't think I ever told you. I think I have a thing for guys who are big and bald."

They laughed. Sam kissed her again, longer this time. Arm in arm, they headed to the stadium gate.

But it turned out that cadets had to sit together during the game, while everyone else was not allowed in the cadet block. It wouldn't do to break up that solid blue mass for TV. Sam was embarrassed and upset at this hurdle thrown upon their first date. But Cheryl hugged him gently and said, "It's OK, honey, we'll meet at halftime. You must admit, this is pretty fitting, considering our affair so far."

"Isn't that the truth," he said.

They walked inside the stadium to the point where they needed to separate. Neither wanted to leave. They hugged and kissed, oblivious to those around them.

"I've got an idea," Sam said. "I'll just find someone to switch clothes with me, and he can sit with the cadets."

But Cheryl just laughed. "Oh, you're brilliant, Sam! I'm sure no one will notice a stranger in their midst like that."

He grinned at her in return. "Well, they're about to kick off," he said. "They told us all to be in place before that. It's not like anyone tells you what to do at the Air Force Academy, right?"

"Right. You all are as free as birds. I don't know what you're complaining about." Cheryl wrapped her arms around his neck and kissed him deeply, lightly touching his tongue with hers. "After the game, you're all mine," she said as she left.

He admired her walking away from him up the steps. Her legs were long, slender, and more beautiful than he remembered, and her taste lingered in his mouth. She turned and smiled at him. He was aroused, but there was nothing he could do about it.

The AFA Falcons beat the Colorado Buffalos. It was a good game, but Sam was distracted to say the least. He was never so desperate to have a football game end.

They only had a few hours to be alone before he needed to get on the academy bus. They spent most of the time necking in her blue Volkswagen Karmann Ghia, which was parked on a hill overlooking the town, while Buffalo Springfield sang "What It's Worth" on her radio.

It was cramped in the Karmann Ghia, and the bucket seats were obstacles, but Sam and Cheryl were both young, flexible, and willing, so neither of them were really deterred. Cheryl did not want things to go too far, and he respected her wishes. The passion was still intense, nonetheless.

When she dropped him off at the bus, he was sweating through his lipstick-stained uniform shirt as he climbed the stairs. As he sat in his bus seat, he felt a chemical bond between them that impelled him to keep striving to get together. But with him being stuck at the academy, they had to be content with more letters and the short occasional call when he was able to find both the time and a private, safe pay phone.

He was released to go home to St. Louis for a few days at Christmas, but Cheryl needed to see her parents, who had recently moved from St. Louis to Seattle. He understood but hated that they would miss the chance to get together. The sight, smell, and feel of her was a sharp memory rather than just a faraway dream.

The next April, Sam and Cheryl saw another chance to get together. By then, he was in the process of resigning, waiting for the authorities to respond to his request. Only a month or so remained before the end of the spring term, when fourth classmen would become actual human beings again. Restrictions had somewhat lessened, and grunts were now able to get a few limited day passes.

She picked him up at the visitor center early on a Saturday morning. They both wanted the day to be as long and as crammed in the company of one another as they could manage. She was leaning against her Karmann Ghia in the parking lot, dressed in a peasant blouse and long skirt.

He ran to her and lifted her up in his arms, kissing and spinning her in a circle.

Leaving the main gate, they were desperate to park at the first secluded place they could find. They found a dirt road not too far out, and Cheryl pulled over a few hundred yards down the path under some trees.

With raspy breath, they pressed their bodies together, and their hands started to explore the ways they could give pleasure to each other. She nibbled at his ear and groaned as his hand travelled up her thigh. They kissed, fumbling with each other's buttons and zippers to release the steam built up over months apart.

With most of their clothes strewn throughout the car, she broke their embrace and crawled between the bucket seats to the backseat. He followed. She wrapped her arms around Sam's neck and kissed him savagely, leaving no doubt about her intentions. He stroked her breasts as she parted her legs and pushed against him. They made love for the first time in the backseat, both lost in their desire.

Afterward, they lay together, naked and twisted, breathing as one. The air was cool, but their bodies radiated enough warmth for comfort. He ran his hand lightly over her abdomen while she brushed his chest with her lips.

"Thank you," he whispered.

"For what? It wasn't like I didn't enjoy myself too."

"Oh, I don't know. Thank you for just being you and loving me."

After they put themselves back together, Sam drove them north on Interstate 25, through Castle Rock and Denver, before turning onto US 36 to Boulder. The crystal air was warming as the sun rose further in the sky. As they approached the town, it glistened in the sun's beams that peaked between the clouds, illuminating the buildings and lighting up the slanting granite ramparts in the mountains behind Boulder. She patted his hand between the seats and gently traced her fingernails up the inside of his arm. Creedence Clearwater sang "Suzie Q" on the car's radio.

"If I live to be a hundred, I'll look back to this day as the greatest in my life," he said.

"I'll bet you say that every day." She leaned over and kissed him on the cheek.

They spent both the morning and afternoon exploring Cheryl's favorite spots. She showed him the campus with its stately brick buildings nestled near the mountains. They visited bookstores and art studios. They strolled through parks and sampled coffee and ate petit sandwiches at sidewalk cafés.

Cheryl's house was on Arapaho Street, away from campus. She pulled the car to the back of the house and parked in the driveway turnaround. They walked to the back door, opened it, and went into the kitchen. The counters were stained beyond any possibility of further cleaning, and the pine cabinets were clearly unfinished. A couch sat a little too low on the living room floor. A large, scratched coffee table made from the top of an old, round dining table sat on cinder blocks in front of the too-low couch, and a bean bag chair rested limply in the corner. He saw a hallway leading away from the living room to the three bedrooms and smelled the sweet scent of women living together with all their beauty products and perfumes.

"Welcome to our garage sale decor," said Cheryl. "We spent a fortune to get this look."

They played cards with her housemates, Jane and Laurie. Both were very friendly, and Sam found their conversations to be amusing and enjoyable. They all had dinner together before Jane and Laurie excused themselves. As soon as they went out the door, Sam and Cheryl jumped into her bed.

After making love, they lay in her bed and talked about her life at CU and Sam's uncertain future. They talked about all the places where they wanted to travel and explore together. They spoke of visiting ancient cities and monuments around the Mediterranean Sea, wineries and walled medieval towns in Europe, and exotic temples in Asia.

"What do you want to be when you grow up?" he asked.

"I know I want to teach, and I love literature, so I'm working on an education degree with a minor in English lit. I picture myself teaching high school English and instilling my own love of language in my students. Who knows? Maybe I'll write some books myself someday." Her face flushed and her eyes sparkled as she talked. "How about you?"

"I wish I knew. It's hard for me to form any clear ones. I'm just trying to figure out who I am and what my dreams are, I guess. I wish I had your focus and your enthusiasm though. It's like you have such a straightforward vision."

"It was pretty easy for me," she said. "My parents are both in education, and they always appeared to be pretty happy with their career choices. That gave me some direction, I suppose. They've just always encouraged me to pursue a profession I love."

"And look at that. It's helped you be the happy, self-confident woman I adore."

She giggled. "Why, thank you."

"What about you?" she asked. "Are your parents good with that sort of thing?"

"Sometimes," he said, "but not so much." Sam pushed the subject of his parents away. "I have to say, when I first met your dad in high school, I was scared shitless of him."

"Why?" she asked. "I didn't know that. He's such a cream puff."

"Yeah, I know that now, but you have to admit he's intimidating when you first see him. He's always been nice to me, though, and it's not like my dad ever exactly asked me to help out when he was working around the house. It was rare, at least. I just was never like that with him, I guess." He turned to her and hugged her, wanting to change the subject. "So . . . how are your parents reacting to us being madly in love instead of being just friends?"

"Mom is just gushing over it. I think Dad's happy, but not yet completely adjusted to this new reality. Maybe he kinda feels like his friend is dating his daughter. He's still trying to figure out how he should treat you."

"I get it. I'm trying to figure out how to act around them too. I was just a harmless best friend before. Now I'm a sex-crazed fiend about to ravage their daughter." He hugged her tighter, grabbing her ass with both hands, and pressed his lips to her neck.

She laughed and raised her chin, offering more of herself. "Ravage away," she said.

As certain and clear as Cheryl's goals were, Sam's were still equally uncertain and murky. He was sure he wanted to complete college, but beyond that, he hadn't a clue. He was so focused on getting back to school and staying out of the draft that few other aspirations had yet materialized. He was not concerned about succeeding in college; he had always been a good student, but he did not yet have any grasp of what he was going to study. Speaking about their plans as a couple was uncomfortable to say the least. Both wanted to be together, and both knew the lives they wanted to lead in the general sense. But it's like they couldn't imagine following any clear-cut paths that would allow them to reach it.

They moved to the living room and became intertwined on the couch, watching the evening news on her black-and-white TV. Walter Cronkite was presenting a news story about Vietnam.

She turned her attention to Sam. "Enough about Vietnam," she said. "Are you excited about getting out of the academy?" she asked. "That is if they ever let you go."

"I'm excited, scared, nervous, and happy all at the same time. I feel like I'm about to explode. You know, I've been thinking," Sam started, sitting up. "Why are we even there? It's a stupid thing for anyone to risk their life over, and I've seen enough already without even having to go there. And if I'm going to become the kind of person they want me to be, I'm not sure I'd even like myself anymore."

She hugged him. "Oh, my poor baby. You do seem tense." She paused. "But you know what? No one else would notice. You act as calm and cool as any cadet should."

They lay together in silence, Cheryl stroking his head. "I, for one, am looking forward to you shedding some of that armor," she said.

"Me too," he answered honestly.

"I think we all have our ways of holding down our negative emotions," Cheryl said softly. "Look, you've been living a stressful life at the academy. You've learned to push all that stuff back. But you can't suppress the lows without also suppressing the highs." She paused. "I think you're coming out of your shell, though."

He hugged her. "Huh. Look at that. You're not just gorgeous, you're wise! Believe me, you've already pulled off a lot of that armor."

They kissed and held it as their bodies pressed together.

As the deadline for starting back to the academy approached, Sam fretted about leaving, knowing he was returning to stress-filled anxiety instead of the comfort of laying in Cheryl's arms. Once back at the academy, he would be sitting idly in his room with nothing to do but worry.

"I can't leave you," he said.

"I don't want you to go either, but what are you going to do? Won't you get in trouble?"

"Probably. But I think I've crossed that bridge already. My situation at the academy has become so bizarre that this doesn't seem like a huge leap to me."

"Well," she said, smiling and patting her thigh. "If you're going to be that way, why don't you just come over here?"

Two days later, they drove back to the academy. He presented his pass to an MP corporal at the gate. The corporal read it, took one look at him and another look at Cheryl. His eyes showed amusement, but his face was impassive. "Pull in and park over there, Cadet Roberts." He pointed to a waiting area inside the gate. "I hope it was worth it."

Sam pulled the car over and parked. The corporal stepped back inside the small building. Sam and Cheryl stewed in the car. The corporal walked to the car and handed Sam a piece of paper. It was a demerit slip for signing in forty-eight hours and ten minutes late on a day pass.

"You can proceed," said the corporal.

Driving through the gate to the visitor center, Sam said to Cheryl, "It sure was."

"As long as they don't throw you in the brig," she said seriously.

It wasn't until later he was told the punishment for being late from a pass: one tour for every five minutes he was late. He did not do the math, but he knew that the consequences for this hooky act with Cheryl, coupled with his other infractions, meant a shitload of marching around with the rifle.

No one at the academy ever mentioned the incident again. But he did get the demerits and was assigned to the tours. It was simply just another thing he wouldn't do willingly.

5 —————————— April 23, 1969

Cheryl and one of her housemates, Laurie, sat in the student union shortly after Sam called to announce his impending release. Cheryl's long auburn hair was tied in a ponytail. Laurie was shorter than Cheryl with curly black hair in a close bob.

Laurie sipped on her soda. "So, what's up with Sam?" she asked. "I thought he was getting out and coming to see you today."

"He's supposed to get released today, but he doesn't know exactly when. He could be on his way by now. If he tried to call me, I wasn't home. It's like we're using smoke signals to communicate."

"Do you know how long he's staying?" Laurie paused a second. "Don't get me wrong, I love the guy too. He can stay as long as he wants."

"I don't think he knows what his next move is," Cheryl said and sighed.

"What's he going to do now that he's out?"

"I don't think he knows that either. He wants to get back in school since he's afraid he'll get drafted."

Laurie reached across the table and patted Cheryl's arm. "Do you know what you're doing?"

Cheryl laughed. "Apparently not. But God, I love him so much, and I know he loves me too." she said. "He would do anything for me. We just fit perfectly together, you know? Bodies, minds, and souls. I feel like we're the same person when we're together."

"Do you agree with him about leaving the academy?"

"I do. I believe his cause is noble. I'm fully behind him."

"Oh, me too," interjected Laurie. "I can definitely see where he's coming from."

Cheryl paused and tears sprang to her eyes. "But I'm so worried about how things will work out with us."

Cheryl's anxiety about Sam was a deep ache in her body. She harbored doubts about whether their love could last if they were separated. She always thought of herself as practical and logical, and logic would be the thing to tell her to break it off. Surely, she could find a more reliable bet in Colorado. But dammit, she loved him too much for that. He was her best friend and lover. She had to stick with him until all possibilities of their love ceased, if it ever would.

She resolved never to express these doubts to him.

Sam's last ride to Boulder came from a University of Colorado student who dropped him near campus in University Hills at about ten o'clock in the morning. He immediately found a pay phone and called Cheryl. She answered on the second ring.

"Sam! Is that you?"

"Yes, honey, it's me."

"I was so worried about you. Where are you?"

"I'm in Boulder, near the campus. I tried to call you last night from Colorado Springs, but there was no answer."

"Well, you're here now, my love." She told him she had a class at eleven and asked him to meet her at a restaurant near campus named the Sink around noon.

Since Sam had some time to kill, he decided to explore. He stashed his bag among the other bags piled up by students outside the shops and restaurants. His own looked like a big mutant version of the other ones, so he thought it would be safe. He began wandering aimlessly around the neighborhood, hoping to work off the excess energy caused by his anticipation of seeing Cheryl.

The neighborhood was just across Broadway Avenue from the campus. He breathed in the warm, sunny air, which was ripe with the smells of pizza, incense, and new plant growth. Large trees were anchored in the root-buckled sidewalks and just beginning to bud. The tree trunks were covered in tacked-up notices announcing upcoming events, goods and services for sale, and noble causes.

Sam watched students carrying books loosely or in hiking packs as they strode along the sidewalks or huddled over outside tables. Most were beautiful—suntanned, dashing, and happy. He could imagine them squeezing in a run on the ski slopes between English and economics.

The men wore their hair in a variety of styles, but most wore it long enough on the sides so that it, at least partially, covered their ears. Long hair seemed to be a badge, proclaiming that you were one of the groovy ones. Sam was painfully aware that the sides of his head were practically shaved, his ears protruding unnaturally. He wanted to integrate himself into this new world as soon as possible, and he felt his short hair identified him as an outsider. He could not wait for it to grow out.

Most women had abandoned the hair spray and curlers of their high school days, letting their hair do whatever it was meant to do. He gazed at their loose locks stirring in the breeze. Sam felt pleasure, excitement, and a deep conviction that he was among the brothers and sisters of his true community. As he walked down the street, people looked him directly in the eyes and gave small, welcoming nods of recognition. He imagined being part of nightly stimulating discussions over beer, wine, and coffee, perhaps going to plays and art house movies.

However, he also sensed his separateness from these people, one beyond the state of his hair. His isolation at the academy had left him on an island in the middle of a river, out of the main flow. He could see the people and events in the mainstream, but as he had not experienced much of it, it felt difficult to relate to those who had. He hadn't lived the same lives as these people over the last year, and it had certainly been an eventful year that had transformed those who were there to see it.

Leaders had been assassinated, race riots had occurred, bitter elections had taken place, and massacres in Vietnam had been committed. Even more sweeping changes in music, fashion, and culture had accelerated beyond Sam. The current of life had passed his island for the last year, never to be lived again, and he had missed it.

Thirteenth Avenue was packed with small shops and restaurants. The sidewalks and patios outside were full of students enthusiastically talking at tables and sipping their drinks. He saw a few shops selling high-end adventure gear and clothes. He imagined himself climbing over mountain peaks in his handwoven Himalayan wool sweater and sleeping in his goose down bag.

There were also more moderately priced establishments around there. Some of these stores sold cheaper new clothing with similar mountain romance. But their merchandise lacked the feeling of self-reliance and high fashion of the higher-priced stuff. Other shops sold used clothing, furniture, kitchen supplies, records, books—all the staples of poor college students. Sam stepped into some of these shops and wandered around like he was a museum tourist.

He bought a tie-dyed T-shirt at a resale clothing store. It was long sleeved and swirled with blues, greens, reds, and yellows of various shades. It had an open collar with three buttons. He considered changing into it. But with his short hair and new jeans, he concluded he might come off as some undercover FBI agent, trying to pass as a hippie. He went into another store and bought a University of Colorado T-shirt and changed out of his air force one in the fitting room.

He walked to the Sink to look it over and find the perfect table. Walking inside the restaurant, he saw that the walls were completely covered with cartoonish drawings, and the ceilings were covered with countless written messages. The drawings reminded Sam of the hippie comic books he had seen. The place felt rich in intellectual and cultural interest while maintaining a comic earthiness.

As his time to meet Cheryl drew near, he selected a table on the sidewalk that provided the widest view. He scanned the crowd, looking for a flash of her auburn hair. A waitress came to the table and smiled at him. She was dark haired, brown eyed, and stunning. She wore a Sink

T-shirt with tattered blue jean shorts, exposing her gorgeous thighs. She was not wearing a bra. Sam felt his heart quicken, his body flushing with rising heat. He tried to appear nonchalant and ordered a glass of water. He was just thinking about how much academy life had turned him into such a horndog when Cheryl appeared behind the waitress.

She wore a T-shirt, also without a bra, over slightly flared blue jeans. Her hair fell over her shoulders and down her chest. The sun sparkled on her fair face as she smiled at Sam. He jumped up and took her in his arms. He felt her body molding against his, her breasts pressing against the bottom of his rib cage.

"Oh baby!" Cheryl whispered.

Their first kiss was long, penetrating, almost aggressive. Then they lightly brushed their kisses over each other's faces, each exploring the feel of the other. He took a deep breath and took in her scent. Though he was becoming more familiar with her, he still felt wobbly in his knees when he held her.

They sat in the sunshine, happily chatting while they sipped 3.2 percent draft beer. They shared a Sink Burger with all the fixings and French fries on the side. The rich, meaty taste of the burger and the sharp crunch of the burger's tomato, pickle, lettuce, and onion filled his mouth. Over time, Sam's nervous anticipation melted into a comfortable sense of togetherness. He felt at peace and so, so lucky to be with her.

6 —————————————————— April 24, 1969

Cheryl and Sam finished their lunch, and he paid the check. They walked further from campus until they reached the parked Karmann Ghia and then drove back to get his bag.

While she drove, he filled her in on his last few days. They spoke about Sam's predicament. He told her how his parents were even more hostile about his decision than he thought they would be and how he was even more worried about catching up on college hours before he got drafted.

"I wish in the worst way that you'd come back to school here and be with me," she said. "I love you."

He reached across the car and placed his hand on her thigh. "I love you too. I want nothing more than to be with you, especially here."

She caressed his hand.

They reached her house and parked in the back. They went through the back door.

Sam laughed and said, "It sure feels different than the last time I was here. It hasn't changed, but I sure have. Can you believe I don't need to take a bus back to the academy now? I'm finally free of all of that, thank God."

She pulled him down the hall to the last door. "You're not *that* free, buddy. This is where you need to get back to." She nodded toward her bedroom door.

They kissed as their bodies merged. She broke the kiss and said, "Did I mention that my housemates are in Denver?"

She opened the door and walked in. Sam grinned and followed her. He wrapped his arms around her and kissed her, marveling at her soft full lips. She broke off the kiss, gasped, then lifted his T-shirt up to his head. She lightly kissed the center of his chest and travelled down to near his navel. Sam exhaled, took the T-shirt off, and threw it on the floor. He pulled her head to his to kiss her, their mouths enveloped. They broke their kiss off again as he removed her T-shirt and wrapped his arms around her. The feel of her naked skin against his was an electric shock of pure excitement. He unzipped her jeans and pulled them and her panties down before she stepped out of them. She pulled down Sam's jeans and underwear herself. He pulled her close, pressing his hips against hers. She pushed hard against him, her lips over his, exploring his mouth with her tongue. He lifted her and let them both fall into her bed.

On her back, Cheryl opened her legs as he urgently pressed his body down on hers. She arched her back and pushed her hips to meet him. He wandered over her breasts with his lips, lightly brushing her skin until goose bumps arose. She wrapped her legs around him, gasping for air, and held his head against her chest as he entered her. The rhythm of their movements started slowly but soon became frantic.

They hardly left the bedroom for three days. Cheryl skipped classes on Thursday and Friday. They lived on beer and anything edible in the apartment. On the few occasions they left the house, they took long walks in the Boulder neighborhoods and inhaled the fragrant spring air. They made love almost every time they touched one another. Even in the mornings, they awoke doing so.

On their third day together, they were laying in her bed while he lightly stroked the skin between her breasts. He lowered his head to her and lightly kissed her right breast just above the nipple. She sighed and gently pushed him away.

"OK, let's get serious," she said. "What're your plans right now?"

"I wish I knew," he answered. "Can I just stay here and be your houseboy?"

Cheryl scowled at him.

"Sorry," he said. "No time for jokes. You know I love you and that I love being here with you. I really don't want to leave you." He threw up his hands in frustration. "I feel like I'm in a maze and can't find my way to you at the end. All I know at this point is that I have to get back in school, or any plans we might have won't mean anything."

"Why can't you stay here a little longer?"

Sam had only completed about half of the class credits for his freshman year. He had to make up those hours in addition to his normal class load, and Selective Service was not going to be patient. The clock was ticking.

"Even if I was enrolled in a school right now, I don't see how I can take enough classes to stay ahead of the draft. I've got to move right now, and I've got to do my best . . . even when it doesn't look like I'll succeed."

"You could take those classes here, couldn't you?"

"If I could afford it. The academy was free. They actually paid me, although after deducting uniforms and other stuff, I haven't actually seen any money yet. And I don't exactly see my parents springing for out-of-state tuition after I let that go. My dad and mom grew up during the Great Depression. They never met a nickel they didn't love. And I don't have time to work first to get the money together before they draft me."

They embraced and stroked each other in silent thought.

"So . . . you're going to leave me," she said.

He tightened his embrace. "Please help me find another way."

She broke away from him and sat up in the bed. "You don't even seem that upset about it. I swear, you're like a machine sometimes, holding back your emotions. You should be scared shitless right now, but you're not showing it." She turned away from him and started crying softly. "It's just so hard for me to reach under that shield of yours and get a reaction from you."

He let her cry as he softly kneaded her shoulder. "I'm sorry, Cheryl."

He reflected on what she had said and knew it was true. He also knew that the dispassionate machinelike behavior was exactly what the air force was shooting for. He pulled Cheryl closer to him and said, "Look, I get it. The Air Force Academy is supposed to train pilots, and cold and calculating is how pilots should be. When shit hits the fan and his pants are on fire, a pilot needs to remain calm to increase the chances of survival, that's all. But the flip side is that it makes you unemotional and clinical. You told me that yourself. I hate what I'm becoming."

She touched his cheek. He continued, "I remember once when I was getting harassed by three upperclassmen. It was called a dress inspection, and they did it in a dorm hall near one of their rooms. I had to show up in fancy parade dress with my rifle. They ordered me to do rifle drills and made me quote airplane specifications and other air force-trivia bullshit while all three were yelling in my ears." He paused. "But the scary part was that, with all of that happening, I found myself thinking about something else at the same time. It's like I could separate myself from the moment."

She pulled her hand back. "That's not normal," she said gently.

"No shit. Don't I know it. When I experienced that emotional detachment, it really scared the hell out of me. I didn't recognize myself. Now I'm scared that I can't relate to anyone outside the academy." He threw his arms around her and held her tightly. "But I know two things: I do love you, and I'll do all I can to get back to you."

She gazed at him adoringly. "There's one thing I've always loved about you, even when we were just friends. You, at your core, are a positive and optimistic person. You roll with the punches and always assume things will work out. You truly believe the world is improving, despite the setbacks." She stroked his arm with her fingertips. "That type of spirit fills me up and comforts me. I just thought you should know," she said. Hugging him against her chest, she held his head in her hands. "I have faith in you, Sam. We'll both do what we can, and I'll wait until things settle down for you."

7 ——————————— March 1, 1969

Last fall, the challenges of boot camp had transitioned into the challenges of academics. Once classes began, the upperclassmen had to ease off slightly on their harassment, likely due to time constraints rather than a new spirit of empathy for Sam's fellow grunts.

But a grunt was a grunt for a year. Fourth classmen were still required to be at attention anytime they were not in their rooms, bathrooms, or the classroom buildings. Even though fourth classmen were allowed to be at ease in their own rooms, their doors had to be open when they were inside, and upperclassmen could enter at any time. The grunt had to then snap to attention and yell out a greeting.

A sprawling stone terrazzo in the middle of the academy was a hub of activity. With their stiff gaits, grunts were only allowed to run on the lighter border stones that bisected the larger areas. They stopped at each corner before cutting the corner with a perfectly square turn.

This terrazzo was called the Blue Zoo by cadets. Tourists on the chapel balcony above viewed the scurrying cadets below. When the entire cadet wing assembled on the terrazzo before marching to meals or in parades, it often became a special tourist attraction.

Sam remembered one parade in particular that included a fighter flyover. Generals from the US and other countries were attending a conference at the academy, so a big show was in order. The entire cadet wing of several thousand stood at attention on the terrazzo—an ordered mass of shining silver and blue.

The fighter, an F-105 Thunderchief, approached the assembled cadets. It flew close to the ground with just enough altitude to clear the mountains behind the academy. Sam did not have to even tilt his head to see the plane coming straight at them. But something was not right. He could see it but not hear it. The plane silently rushed at them. When it was almost overhead, the jet sound finally hit, followed almost immediately by a huge boom above the roar of the engine. Sam felt the air stir from the sonic boom, causing some of the glass sides of the surrounding buildings to shatter.

The military bigwigs attending the conference were just inside several of those areas, and some were slightly injured for it. The crowd on the chapel balcony definitely got more than they came for that day. They were dazed, but thankfully unhurt.

An investigation determined that the plane was flying slightly faster than the speed of sound when it passed over the academy, causing the sonic boom. The plane's flight speed indicator was found to have read low. For all the pilot knew he had been flying below the speed of sound, rather than above it. He was exonerated. Since the tourists were more entertained than scared, there was no great harm. And even the generals took it in stride.

The real trouble came with the upper-class pressure at meals. The academy dining hall was a cavernous structure, capable of seating all several thousand cadets at once. Sam was awed by the massive open space and huge balcony at the head of the room, large enough to seat a multitude of higher-ranked cadets, air force staff officers, and other dignitaries.

Each long table on the cadet floor sat twelve. Sam was one of three fourth classmen who sat at one end. They were required to sit on the last six inches of their chairs while at attention. When eating, they ate "square meals," involving squared-off, robot-like movements, lifting food to their mouths mechanically. Half of the food didn't even make it to their mouths because their eyes had to be always focused on their plates. They were required to raise their eyes when spoken to, usually when they were being quizzed by an upperclassman on air force trivia. With a nine-to-three ratio of upper to lower classmen, the questioning was constant. Sam never had enough to eat and was always hungry. He had been skinny in high school but lost another fifteen pounds at the academy.

After each meal, the grunts would zigzag back across the terrazzo to their rooms. Upperclassmen pounced like cats on the poor souls who had spilled food on themselves. After receiving their fair share of abuse, these grunts were sent on their way, shouting, "I bombed myself, sir!"

All infractions, no matter how minor, caused immediate intimidation and abuse by the upperclassmen. They could not normally touch a grunt without his permission. But they *could* get in his face and scream at the top of their lungs and make him drop for pushups at practically any moment. And it didn't stop there.

Upperclassmen could inspect the grunts or their dorm rooms at any time. Their personal appearance had to be perfect, with shoes spit polished to a mirror finish, their hat at just the right angle, and everything tucked in tight. They cleaned every surface in their room to survive white-gloved probing for dust in hidden places, using toothpaste to make their bathroom shine. Their beds had to be made with perfect square corners, drawn tight enough to bounce a coin. Some cadets slept on top of their covers to help preserve their pristine condition.

Sam and Derek had spent many hours in their room discussing the lunacy of these games. Even though Derek was president of their class, he was contemptuous of the system. They both still felt respect for the military, despite the filtered, infrequent, and still-troubling news from Vietnam. But they doubted that the goal at the end of the academy lunacy, when they became upperclassmen and later officers, was worth it. Even though they agreed being upperclassmen was an improvement, they both felt it was still a restricted life in a world that seemed to be expanding and evolving all around them all the time. And it seemed like they were being left behind by it.

A lot of the time, they talked about military life after graduation from the academy. What bothered them both was the complete control the military exercised. In the civilian world, you could always quit if your job was unbearable, as was your right. But that wasn't the case in the military. You could not just quit. You could request a transfer, but your superiors had the power to approve or deny it.

There was a possibility that was even worse. If you were being ordered to perform an act in combat to which you objected or had moral qualms about, you could not refuse without possibly going to the brig or experiencing other consequences, like a dishonorable discharge. Consequences like these could ruin your entire life. It was clear by their conversations that Sam and Derek were both very uncomfortable with that level of unbridled authority over them.

Any cadet who left the academy in his first or second year owed no further service to the air force, but he could still be drafted by the army or marines if he could not get another draft deferment. With a cadet who left his third or fourth year, however, he still owed two years as an enlisted man in the air force. Since Derek came to the academy from the regular air force, he would need to serve out the rest of his enlistment in the regular air force as if he had never attended the academy at all.

But Sam did not feel too sorry for him. Derek had somehow negotiated for his new assignment as a recreation sergeant at Travis Air Force Base near San Francisco, which he would take part in once his discharge from the academy was final. He seemed pleased with this, saying he would be counting volleyballs and soaking up San Francisco's culture. Sam wondered again what Derek held over some people. He was as untouchable as an underworld kingpin.

Neither Sam nor Derek had any doubts that they would eventually be released from the academy. Their uncertainty was simply over how painful the air force would make it, and how they might be punished afterward.

8 ———————————— April 26, 1969

Sam sat silently in the passenger seat as Cheryl drove the Karmann Ghia down the desolate road near Lafayette, Colorado. He stared morosely ahead while she occasionally sniffed back her tears.

"You know you can't drive me all the way to St. Louis," he said. "As much as I want to stay with you, we're only prolonging our misery here."

With a short sob, she pulled the car onto the shoulder of the road. He opened his door; stepped out onto the cold, desolate prairie; and pulled his seatback forward. As he wrestled his bag out of the backseat and placed it on the ground, Cheryl ran around to his side of the car and fiercely wrapped her arms around him. Her whole body shook as she cried. He could not talk and could only try to communicate his love through his embrace. He could not remember ever being so miserable and sad. She broke away, tried to wipe the tears from her eyes, and got back in the car. She made a U-turn and drove away.

He stood waiting for a ride after she left. Feeling that all energy and the air itself had been removed from him, he watched the few cars on the road pass him without slowing down. Several hours passed. Storm clouds were beginning to form to the west of him beyond the mountains. It was colder, and the still air began to stir.

He flinched at a short, high-pitched squeak about ten feet behind him. Curious, he snapped his head around toward the sound but saw nothing. There was a squeak to his right, followed by one on his left. Several prairie dogs appeared at their tunnel entrances and seemed to mock him with squeaks for his jumpiness before they ducked back underground.

He laughed. He felt disconnected from reality. He had to marvel at the absurdity of standing alone on an open plain, surrounded by prairie dogs, just having lost his girlfriend, and being chased by a storm. At the same time, he couldn't help but feel a small creep of thrill at the idea of discovery.

Sam shook his head in bewilderment and said, "How in the hell did I get here?"

The wind picked up as the darkness fell. It started to sleet, tapping on the ground and stinging Sam's face. He raised his coat hood and faced east, shielding his face from the wind and ice.

Sam heard the low rumble of a car with a questionable exhaust system in the distance behind him. He turned and saw headlights off to the west, moving fast toward him. When the car rushed by him, the driver hit the brakes and skidded onto the shoulder. When it did, Sam saw a copper-colored Buick Riviera steaming on the roadside gravel. As he dragged his bag to the car, he heard the sleet hitting and hissing on the Buick's hood and saw the falling ice sparkle in its taillights.

A young Hispanic man opened the driver-side door, got out, and ran to the back of the car. He hit the trunk lock with his fist and the trunk popped open, revealing a disarray of clothes. He threw Sam's bag on top.

"Hola, hombre," the young man shouted as he slammed the trunk down. He looked to be about Sam's age.

"Hola," said Sam and followed him around to the passenger's side.

The man opened the door. Latin music was playing on an eight-track cassette player in the car's stereo. He saw an attractive Hispanic girl in the front passenger seat and another boy and girl in the backseat. They all appeared to be in their teens.

"I'm Rico," said the driver, holding out his hand. They shook, and Rico pulled the seat's back forward as the girl slid to the front of the seat. "Afraid you'll have to squeeze in, amigo."

The girl in the back seat slid to the left to make room. She had to squeeze against the boy to do so. The car had an attractive, but useless, metal ornamental plate with the Buick logo right in the center of the seat's back, making this middle seat unpractical for anyone to sit on. But the boy seemed to be more than content with this, as he looked pleased at the close attention of the girl. Sam thought they looked cozy.

He climbed in. "My name is Sam. Glad to meet you all."

Rico climbed in and pointed to the girl next to him.

"This beauty is Carla. Your friends back there are Julio and Roxanna. I hope you can tell who's who."

"I think so," said Sam.

Rico was slightly built, but his movements communicated strength and grace. His black hair was combed straight back, and black stubble graced his chin. He was a few inches shorter than Sam. Rico spoke with a slight accent but with better English grammar than Sam thought he himself used.

Across the Riviera's wide center console from Rico, Carla sat prettily and primly in the front passenger seat. Her straight black hair hung to her shoulders, and Sam observed her fine features and light copper skin as she turned to glance at him.

"Hello, Sam," Carla said.

Her strong, flowery scent filled the air.

"Hi, Carla."

He looked across the bench seat at Julio and Roxanna. Roxanna was pretty like Carla, but her face was fuller and more girlish. Julio looked slightly younger than Rico. Where Rico was lean, Julio still carried some of his boyish pudginess, and his face was smooth from any of the stubble on Rico.

Sam nodded his head. "Roxanna . . . Julio . . . So glad to meet you."

They answered, "Hi," in unison.

"Thanks so much for stopping for me. It was getting ugly out there."

"We're glad to help," said Carla.

"*Ándale, ándale!*" shouted Rico as he slammed the gear shift into drive and mashed down the accelerator pedal. The engine roared as the tires spun in the gravel. The car lurched forward and started to fishtail in the gravel before Rico got control and moved the car onto the pavement. He kept his foot down on the pedal, and the Riviera kept accelerating, pushing Sam back in his seat. Sam looked at the speedometer and saw it steadily climbing. In seconds, they were going ninety mph.

Rico settled for the newfound speed and let off on the accelerator. Sam wondered how long they would survive driving ninety mph in the sleet.

"Are you all in a hurry?" asked Sam.

"Funny you should ask," said Julio. "Why yes, we are."

He pointed to Carla and Roxanna.

"We're late getting to their cousin's quinceañera in Cheyenne Wells."

"What's a quinceañera?" asked Sam.

Rico explained, "In Mexican culture, it's a coming-of-age party for fifteen-year-old girls. Family and friends gather from far and wide. It's a grand celebration. The girl of honor dresses like Cinderella. There's lots of music, dancing, and eating. The men sneak out back and sip something stronger than the iced tea and lemonade offered inside."

"Sounds fun. Why are you late?" asked Sam.

"We're from Bakersfield, California," said Carla. "Rico had a baseball game, so we were late getting started. We've been driving straight through for about eighteen hours, just stopping for gas and snacks."

Sam glanced out his window at the blur of fence posts in the slanting sleet. He was grateful that at least the roads were straight and flat.

"Rico is my brother," said Julio.

"And Carla is my cousin," said Roxanna.

Sam tilted his head as he thought about that.

"Don't worry," said Rico. "What's important is the girls are not related to the boys . . . at least, as far as we know."

Carla gently slapped Rico on the arm.

"What do all of you do back home?" asked Sam.

"We were all born there," Carla said, gesturing around the three of them. "Some of our families work at the chicken processing plant, some work at restaurants, grocery stores, car repair shops, farms, you name it. We're all still in high school, but we also have second jobs."

Rico said, "Most of our parents came to California from Mexico to work in the fields in the late fifties or early sixties. Some went back, some stayed."

"What do you do, Sam?" asked Roxanna.

Sam hesitated. "That's a long story. I'm going home to look into getting back in college." He hesitated. "I quit the Air Force Academy last week, and I'm hitchhiking to St. Louis. I hope to get back in school after I get there."

"Whoa, cowboy!" exclaimed Julio. "Why'd you do that?"

"I just wasn't cut out to be a career officer in the air force," Sam answered simply.

This was the same answer he used over and over for questioning officers during his six-week limbo awaiting release. The words sprang from his mouth without him even thinking about them.

Rico reached down and popped out the Latin music cassette and popped another cassette into the eight-track player. He pushed a button, and The Doors' song "Hello, I Love You" blared from the speakers.

The Buick Riviera sped across the countryside. The sleet had subsided, and Sam felt a little safer. The sky was darkening further as night took hold.

Sam asked, "What are all of your plans after high school?"

Roxanna shrugged. "I guess I'll work at my aunt's beauty shop. She always needs people. Either that or be a waitress."

She looked down.

Carla turned her head to look between the seats and beamed. "I'm going to be on TV. I've been practicing to be a weather girl." She flashed her teeth in a wide smile and pointed her arms becomingly toward an imaginary weather screen. "Tonight," she said with exaggerated enthusiasm, "we expect it to be dark with a slight chance of hail, sleet, or snow." She giggled.

"Nice," said Sam, grinning. "I can see that."

He believed Carla could do it. She had just the right combination of good looks, intelligence, and friendly confidence. And he realized he had found out quite quickly he just liked being around her. This charisma would likely shine through the TV.

Julio said, "I work in my dad's garage after class. I hope to get into some tech school and learn all about mechanics, maybe even start my own shop."

Sam said, "It would be nice to run your own business. You like the work?"

"Your hands are always dirty, but I like fixing things that break, helping people out."

Sam looked into the rearview mirror, which reflected the top of Rico's face.

"What about you, Rico?"

Rico hesitated. "I dunno . . . If I'm lucky, I'll get a scholarship to play football somewhere." He paused. "If not, I sure don't want to work at Julio's garage." Julio swatted Rico's head. "What does it matter, anyway? I'll probably get drafted into the army whatever I do."

"I hear you," said Sam. "Leaving the academy has left my ass hanging out. If I can't get back in school quickly, I'll be way behind in semester hours and lose my college deferment."

"There aren't any deferments out there for people like us, man," Julio said. "We can't afford to go to college. Why do you think there are so many black dudes and Mexican-Americans like us who get drafted?"

There was an uncomfortable silence. Sam felt like a self-centered ass.

"Sorry, Julio," said Sam. "I know I've been fortunate to be able to go to college. I guess I just have the family that always had the expectation that we'd all be able to get a degree, and I've had great teachers to help me along the way. I was lucky." He paused a moment. "But it looks like I might fuck all of that up anyway."

Rico reached under his seat and brought out a large bottle of tequila. He unscrewed the cap and raised the bottle in a toast.

"Fuck 'em. Here's to our plans . . . or to our lack of 'em."

"To our plans!" the others shouted.

Rico raised the bottle to his lips and took a long swallow. He shivered and passed the bottle to Carla. Carla took a small sip and puckered up her face. She passed the bottle to Sam, who took a swig and offered it to

Roxanna. Roxanna shook her head, so Sam handed it to Julio.

Only two rounds later, Julio hit the back of Rico's seat and shouted, "We can't fight in that fuckin' war. You can't tell the good guys from the bad guys. What does Vietnam have to do with us, anyway?"

Sam felt the soft buzz of the tequila. "You know, I really don't think this is like World War II," he said. "Back then, our country was directly threatened by these vile assholes. Hell, the whole world was threatened by vile assholes. I like to think I would have stood up and proudly fought in that one."

Julio had possession of the bottle and raised it in salute to Sam's words. "You got it, man. I'm sure there are plenty of assholes in Vietnam, but I don't see any of them coming here to take our freedom and rape our women, you know?" He took another swig to emphasize the point.

Everyone was silent and listened to the eight-track player. Jim Morrison's "People are Strange" sang on.

Rico said, "I dunno, Sam. You gotta be careful, man. If you go over there, you better hope some gung-ho sergeant doesn't find out you resigned from the Air Force Academy and puts a bullet in your head during a firefight."

Sam thought for a few seconds. "Thanks for putting that picture in my head, Rico. But I guess I don't doubt it could happen."

They started another round of the tequila as the Riviera thundered down the road.

The Selective Service System was currently drafting about twenty thousand young men every month. All males were required to register when they turned eighteen. Soon after, each young man received a letter informing him of his status. For a giant government institution, Selective Service was very efficient.

It was not a lottery. Basically, a young man was eligible to be drafted unless he had some deferment to shield him. There were numerous deferments, but two of the most common were 4F for men with physical limitations or medical conditions and 2S for full-time students, commonly called the college deferment. A young man could claim to be a conscientious objector, but he practically needed to be an established monk to qualify for that.

Without a deferment, or when a deferment ceased to be valid anymore, Selective Service would take a few months to notice and would then reclassify the young man's status to 1A. Being 1A meant that he could be instructed at any time to report to the nearest Selective Service center for a physical.

Unless he flunked the physical or could appeal the 1A classification, he was then told to report on a certain day and climb onto a bus to boot camp. These days, it seemed likely that the young man was then going to Vietnam just after training. Sam even feared that once his name came up, the army would see that he had already passed an even tougher boot camp and would just ship him straight over to Vietnam.

And, of course, the US Marines siphoned off some of the draftees. The possibility of ending up in the Marines added a little more dread to the pile already caused by the draft. Leaving the Air Force Academy and landing in the marines would definitely qualify as jumping out of the frying pan and into the fire. Some 1A men threw up their hands and tried to voluntarily enlist in the navy or air force, seeking a branch of the military less likely to kill them.

Because a cadet at the Air Force Academy was as much a college student as a member of the real air force, Sam had a 2S deferment. To keep that deferment, he needed to complete thirty-two semester hours per year. He had not completed his spring semester at the academy, and he would not be able to enroll anywhere before summer. Not all of his academy credits would transfer to a new school. Most schools did not give a shit about Military Science 101, much less grant semester hours for taking it. Such credits were erased. As a result, Sam was far behind and had no idea how he would catch up. He felt a wave of panic every time he thought about it. He could not foresee a path forward, and without Cheryl, he could not look forward to a better future.

Carla turned to look back between the seats at Sam. "You have any regrets about leaving the academy?"

"I miss my friends. Some are like brothers. I also regret not getting an F-4 Phantom fighter jet with my name on it."

Carla giggled. "That would be fun. Zipping around in your own jet. But you wouldn't want to hurt anyone with it, right?"

"No, I wouldn't. I guess that's part of the problem."

Sam walked beside Captain Turner on the tarmac of Peterson Field in Colorado Springs. The odor of jet fuel hung in the air, and the high-pitched roar of jet engines made normal conversation impossible. He and Turner were both wearing one-piece flight suits and carried their helmets with oxygen masks under their arms. Parachutes were strapped to their bodies, making walking somewhat awkward.

They approached a T-33 training jet sitting on the tarmac. A small ground crew was scampering over the sleek plane, preparing it for flight. The clear canopy was tilted back, revealing two pilot seats, one behind the other. The jet had large openings on each side under the cockpit to suck in air for the single jet engine in the tail, and the wings extended straight out from the plane's fuselage to the two fuel tanks mounted at the ends of the wings. The T-33 had been modified for training purposes from its earlier role as the F-80 Shooting Star fighter. Sam thought it was a magnificent-looking plane.

All of the fourth-class cadets were taking rides in the T-33s. Sam suspected that in addition to providing the cadets with a motivational experience, it was also a shakedown flight. The air force wanted to identify those who couldn't handle the flight, likely making them unsuitable as pilots.

Sam loved to fly. He was eight years old when he first flew. His family traveled across the Pacific to Taiwan to live there. The island-skipping trip was on a giant Pan American Boeing 377 Stratocruiser: a fat, propeller-driven plane sporting two passenger levels. He was enthralled during the takeoff and had his nose pressed against the window during most of the flight as well as the landings in Hawaii, Guam, Tokyo, and finally Taipei. Armed-forces officers routinely flew first class with their families when they were relocating to a new assignment. First-class seats on the Pan Am Stratocruiser were expansive. At night, a beautiful flight attendant folded out Sam's seat into a bed, covered with luxurious linens and a warm blanket. She tucked him in, and he drifted into deep sleep, listening to the propeller engines drone.

As an air force attaché at the American embassy in Taiwan, his father was also the pilot of the embassy plane, an air force C-47 Skytrain outfitted for passenger use. Sam and the rest of his family sometimes filled empty seats and went along to exotic spots throughout Asia. His dad often allowed Sam to sit in the copilot seat next to him. Occasionally, he even let Sam take the wheel as he pointed out the dizzying array of instruments and controls throughout the cockpit.

That had been exciting for a little boy, but now he was stepping into a fighter jet, which made the C-47 seem like a slow bus. Sam's body tingled with anticipation.

Captain Turner walked around the jet, making notations on a clipboard. Sam followed him.

Turner yelled in his Texan drawl above the noise, "If you're going to fly a plane, you need to check everything out yourself. 'Oops' doesn't cut it up there, and it's a long way down."

When he was satisfied, Turner pointed to the ladder leading to the cockpit.

"Well, cadet, time to climb aboard, if you're still with me."

"Absolutely, sir!" Sam yelled.

He climbed the ladder hanging from the open cockpit. One of the flight crew, a corporal, followed him up the ladder and guided him into the rear seat. There was barely enough room for his legs, which the stick was wedged between. The console ahead of him was crammed with even more instruments. The corporal fastened the thick seatbelt and shoulder harnesses. He then showed Sam how to put on his helmet and oxygen mask, connecting the plane's hose to it.

With the helmet on, he heard the faint hiss of airflow and the corporal's voice on the speakers inside his helmet. "You breathing alright?" Sam nodded. "Good, you can let the mask hang until you take off." Sam did as the corporal suggested. "If you have to puke, pull your mask down and use the barf bag in front of you. You don't want to smell that shit in your mask all the way home. And I don't want to clean it out of the cockpit either."

"Understood," said Sam, wondering what was in store for him.

The corporal gave him a thumbs up.

Captain Turner had climbed into the front seat and was going over the preflight checklist. The flight crew lowered and locked the canopy, lessoning the outside din of jet engines.

Turner started the engine, which more than replaced the outside noise. Sam felt the engine vibration through his seat. He looked to both sides and up through the clear canopy, excited but feeling exposed.

Sam heard Turner on the radio.

"Peterson Tower, this is Bravo Three Niner requesting taxi clearance to runway Alpha Two Zero."

"Bravo Three Niner, this is Peterson Tower. Proceed to runway Alpha Two Zero and await takeoff instructions."

"This is Bravo Three Niner, acknowledged," Turner stated.

The pitch of the engine rose, and the plane started to roll with it. It gathered speed as Turner guided the plane along the taxiway. He slowed down as he approached the end of it and turned the plane to face down the runway before stopping.

"Peterson Tower, this is Bravo Three Niner. Requesting clearance for takeoff."

"Bravo Three Niner, this is Peterson Tower. You are cleared for takeoff."

"Peterson Tower, this is Bravo Three Niner. Acknowledge cleared for takeoff," drawled Turner. "Cadet Roberts, put your mask on and hold on to your jockey shorts. Here we go."

The engine roared and pulled against the brakes that had held the jet in place. Moments later, Turner released them. The T-33 lunged down the runway, continuing to accelerate. Sam was pressed against his seat and heard his rapid breathing in his mask. The power of the engine vibrated through the metal surrounding him. In almost no time, the jet's nose rose and then the rear wheels left the runway.

Turner pulled back on the stick, and the plane's nose pointed almost straight up into the sky. The engine screamed. Sam felt his weight against the seat increase until he could barely move his head or arms.

"Holy shit!" yelled Sam over the radio.

Turner just chuckled.

Once they reached altitude, Turner eased the plane out of the climb, and they flew level for a while. Sam marveled at the panoramic view through the canopy. He could clearly see the mountains in the west abruptly changing to prairie in the east. Turner took the T-33 through some turns. Some gentle, some not so much. With the jet banked into the turns, Sam saw the ground rush by through the side of the canopy.

"You want to take the stick?" asked Turner.

Sam's excitement grew.

"Yes, sir," he replied.

"Just don't make any drastic moves with it. It's pretty sensitive."

Sam took the stick in his right hand. He was afraid to move it at first, but then gently maneuvered the plane through gradual turns and altitude changes, following Turner's directions. Gradually, he became more comfortable with the controls, making wider turns and faster changes in altitude.

"Good job," said Turner. "Now let me show you how to really fly." Sam felt Turner take the stick back as he released it.

The plane rapidly rolled several times. Sam saw the sky and ground spin around him as he looked up out of the canopy. Turner made a hard right turn and then plunged into a steep dive. Sam became lighter in weight and a little disoriented, but he was having the time of his life. This was nothing like the flying he had experienced before.

Turner leveled off again. For the next forty-five minutes, they cruised over and between mountains, sometimes close enough to see individual trees on the slopes and ridges. Sam felt a hint of the feelings of power and speed that Turner must be experiencing while piloting the plane.

"It's about time we headed back," Turner said. "You want to do a strafing run first?"

Now that sounded exciting.

"Why not, sir."

The T-33's engine pitch rose as it climbed until they were high above the mountain peaks. Turner levelled the plane off.

"Ready or not," said Captain Turner.

The jet rolled 180 degrees and stopped belly-up so that the ground was above Sam's head. They flew like this for several moments. Sam was just starting to adjust to flying upside down, when the plane abruptly fell toward earth. Sam was weightless as the ground rushed at him from above his head. Air turbulence rocked the plane, and it shuddered as it fell. Time slowed down as the adrenaline pumped through his body, and he couldn't help but wonder how long they were going to fall. The ground sure was getting uncomfortably close.

Without warning, Turner simultaneously flipped the plane back over, raised the nose, and fully accelerated. Sam instantaneously changed from weightless to helplessly pinned to his seat. He felt his mask being pulled against its straps and away from his face by the g-forces.

The contents of his stomach suddenly erupted into his throat. He had no time to lower his mask or reach for the barf bag. He kept his mouth closed and swallowed, coughing violently into his mask.

"How you doin' back there, cadet?" Turner asked.

"Just peachy, sir," croaked Sam.

Turner laughed.

The flight back to Peterson Field was uneventful aside from Sam attempting to get the putrid taste of vomit out of his mouth. Turner handed the stick over to Sam a few times. Sam became more accustomed to the feel of the controls and began to execute more and more abrupt moves. Too soon, they were back at Peterson Field. Turner landed the T-33 smoothly and taxied to the tarmac. The canopy opened, and one of the flight crew gave Sam his hand and pulled him upright. Sam's knees wobbled, and his legs felt like they did not belong to him as he lowered himself down the ladder. Captain Turner was standing on the ground and gave him a thumbs up. Sam approached him. "Thank you for the flight, sir. But be honest with me, Captain Turner, sir," Sam yelled. "I'll bet you can't hit shit if you strafe something like that."

Turner grinned in return.

Sam later learned that the pilots had placed a side bet for a case of beer on which of them could make the most cadets throw up. That pilot also gained the honorable title of Prince of Puke.

He was relieved he was not one of those cadets, even though it was close. Instead, he found himself even more eager to fly.

At the academy, there were squadron meetings when the squadron officer—a real air force officer—briefed the cadets on Vietnam missions. These meetings usually occurred in a large room in a section of the dorm where the squadron was housed. A large banner hung behind a speaker's podium that bore the squadron's symbol: the helmeted head of a medieval knight with flames on one side and a flying missile on the other.

Major Fred Collins was Sam's squadron officer. Collins had recently returned from Vietnam, where he was a Wild Weasel pilot. His missions involved flying with his backseat weapons officer over North Vietnamese antiaircraft missile sites. They would transmit a radar signature, which made them look like a big, juicy bomber to the missile site, hoping that the site would lock their radar on them or perhaps even fire a missile. Collins would then evade the projectile and dive down to take out the missile site instead.

Major Collins played audio tapes of some of his missions, which were the radio conversations between him and his weapons officer.

"We have a radar lock from a missile site," his weapons officer calmly stated on the tape.

"Missile fired," he stated a few moments later with a little more tension in his voice.

The roomful of cadets held their breath as the voices went silent. After several moments, the weapons officer said, "We have target lock on the missile site. You can evade any time."

After a few moments of silence, the weapons officer talked, starting calmly, then getting more tense as the moments dragged on. "Any time . . . any time . . . Sweet Jesus, how 'bout now, Fred?!"

"Holy *shiiit!*" he then yelled.

The weapons officer's voice lost its professional demeanor, rising in pitch. High g-forces from the plane's sudden and jarring evasive moves caused the tape machine to change speed, making his voice sound like a chipmunk's.

After several seconds, Collins reported in a normal tone, "Missile evaded."

The weapons officer said, "Target still locked. Missile away," his voice still slightly shaky from the close call. After several more seconds once he gathered himself, he said, "Direct hit. Target destroyed."

Major Collins told the cadets that the missile fired at them needed to get very close before they tried to fake it out. If they waited long enough, the missile could not turn fast enough and would miss them. Duck too soon, you were toast. Sam doubted he had the nerves and steady hand to fly those missions every day.

Major Collins would sometimes show the cadets mission films taken from other aircraft cameras, mounted below the plane's fuselage. The jungle rushed by in the overhead view, occasionally showing roads and villages, until the flash of explosives erupted in the image. The fire spread as the plane continued to fly overhead, sometimes completely enveloping the jungle view on the camera.

The cadets would ooh and aah during the bomb bursts. Sam joined right in. But later he could not help thinking of the terror and pain of those on the ground experiencing that fire-filled hell.

10 ———————————— April 26, 1969

Like most boys, Sam had grown up playing war with his friends. At times when he didn't own a toy gun, he would make do with a stick as a substitute rifle. Their mock battles raged through the woods near his neighborhood. They built elaborate forts within fallen trees. Sometimes they pretended to be World War II soldiers, sometimes cowboys and Indians. At the pool, Sam pretended to be a frogman, secretly swimming underwater to attach imagined bombs on the hulls of conceived enemy ships.

The Air Force Academy provided the opportunity to play soldier like never before. They issued every cadet his own M1 rifle—a highly polished, working one carried by soldiers in World War II. The cadets marched with them, learned rifle drills, and charged through the woods firing blanks at each other on military exercises. The cadets were also trained on the range with the most modern M16 rifles and various handguns. Sam found he enjoyed that.

Partly out of trying to please his father, and partly out of a respect for the military, Sam had entered the screening process for nomination to the academy. The process involved a battery of written tests, athletic exhibitions, and physical prodding. There were meetings where films were shown, highlighting the academy's beautiful surroundings and Boy Scout camp activities. The films also showed slick, sexy jets blasting across the sky, just to show the boys how cool the air force's own toys could be.

Admission to the Air Force Academy, just like West Point and the Naval Academy, was gained through appointment by each state's senators and congressmen. The president also filled some slots, such as for military sons. In practice, all applicants were fed into one screening process, and the authorities tried to match the top competitors with whatever appointment slot that fit. Sam was not that enthusiastic about attending a male-only military school. But he figured that with only the president, senators, and congressmen making appointments, his chances were not that great anyway. It was important to his dad, so he humored him. He applied to six other schools and was accepted at four.

It seemed that he woke up one morning and was at the academy. This had happened only three weeks after graduation. President Lyndon B. Johnson had appointed him. He took in his surroundings in a daze and soon realized he had probably made a mistake.

Where had he gone wrong? The aim of becoming a pilot was not incentive enough. This was no boyhood wargame. This was preparation for a real war, for a cause he did not support. Was his opposition to the war based on moral grounds or self-preservation? Probably a mix of both. Sam thought such doubts and a lack of commitment during combat might also make you hesitate. That could get you killed. Maybe evolution favored those creatures who either immediately ran away from danger or fought it, rather than those who thought about the choice first.

He knew that much of his motivation to leave the academy was not so noble. College was supposed to be fun, dammit. The Air Force Academy was the opposite. He yearned to take part in the good times and to connect with the riveting people he knew were somewhere out there.

And out there they were. Rico pulled the Riviera in front of the Mountain Vista Motel in Burlington, Colorado. Their neon sign buzzed in the dark, the t in motel still dark. The sign also proclaimed that they offered free TV and local phone calls.

"You need a warm, safe place to sleep," declared Carla. "Let's get you checked in before we leave."

They all got out of the car and hugged Sam. Rico and Carla followed him into the motel lobby. The desk clerk eyed them suspiciously but took Sam's money and gave him a key. "I'll give you the kitchenette suite," he said.

Carla hugged him again.

"Hang in there, hombre," said Rico, shaking Sam's hand.

Sam thanked them for the ride. As they left the motel, Sam began to drag his bag toward his room. He heard the rumble of the Riviera as they headed south toward Cheyenne Wells. He silently wished them luck. They were good kids, facing some of the same uncertainties he faced. He suddenly felt a rush of thankfulness for the advantages that he had that they did not.

Sam was not tired, so he just threw his bag into his room and went outside. The motel was near the center of Burlington. The street was dimly lit, and a partial moon glowed through the moving clouds. Old brick buildings lined the street. Some had been restored, but a few were still boarded up. The air was cool, and there was a light breeze, causing the small trees planted alongside the sidewalk to stir. Crickets chirped, and he could smell dirt from the freshly plowed fields near the town. Two blocks away, he spotted a neon sign on a newer building blinking, COWBOY BOB'S. He thought the walk might cut through the tequila fog in his head. Cowboy Bob's did not look like a 3.2 percent beer joint where someone under twenty-one could legally drink in Colorado, so he hoped they would not card him. He decided to take the chance, walked down the street, and approached the bar.

He opened the door and entered. It was dark and smoky. Marty Robbins sang "I Walk Alone" from the jukebox. Sam walked across an open space where several cowboys were playing pool. High tables and chairs surrounded the pool tables and a dance floor. A long bar stretched along the back of the room. Dancing couples swayed to Marty Robbins's wailing lament on being left alone. Sam could relate.

He stepped up to the bar and took a stool at the corner. A young blonde girl stood behind the bar, dressed in a short skirt, cowboy boots, and a cowboy shirt left open enough to show off her cleavage. She beamed at him.

"What can I get you, darlin'?" she asked.

He hesitated to consider whether beer on top of tequila was a good idea or whether another shot of tequila would do him in for good. "Do you have Coors?" he asked finally.

"Whatta ya think, honey? Isn't this Colorado?" she said and laughed. She took a tall glass from the countertop and placed it under the tap. She opened it, expertly stopping just before the head overflowed. She positioned it on the bar in front of him, finishing it off with a wink and a smile. "Now you enjoy that, darlin.'"

Before he could engage her any further, she left to tend to another customer. He sipped on his beer. The beer's bubbles were released in his mouth along with its bittersweet taste. He turned his back to the bar and surveyed the room. The crowd ranged from just-legal to people in their fifties. Most were couples on dates or part of larger groups partying together. A few of the tables were filled with what looked like single girls, which were constantly being buzzed by what looked to be single boys. Conversation and laughter sometimes drowned out Marty Robbins.

He felt the community celebration of life on the plains. These people knew each other's history. They shared each other's daily schedules and tasks. Their kids went to school and played together. It was clear they were regulars here.

The jukebox finished its song. The bar's front door opened, and a young hippie couple came in. They both had long straight hair down to their shoulders. The woman hesitated at the door and looked around, holding the man back. The talk and laughter from the crowd diminished. The long-haired man huddled with the woman in conversation before he evidently convinced her to come further into the room. They walked toward a table. Haltingly, some of the bar conversation started back up.

Just as the noise in the bar was returning to normal, one of the cruising single guys turned to the couple and bellowed, "Look, guys! Look what we got. We sure have a pair of cuties here!"

Most of the crowd laughed. There was no humor in the sound, and it was edged with viciousness, laughing at the couple and not with them.

Sam was reminded of a cruel classroom ridiculing an awkward student for giving a wrong answer. The atmosphere turned from communal congeniality to communal threat. He heard mutterings from the crowd about the couple's right to be in there with the rest of them.

The hippies stopped walking toward the table, hesitating, then turned and went back out the door. The crowd laughed even harder. Sam tossed down the rest of his beer. The urge to meet new people had dissolved. He left a big tip for the bartender and left Cowboy Bob's.

11 ———————— April 26, 1969

Walking back to the motel, Sam thought of his father. When he had announced that he was going to resign, his dad had exploded. He was convinced that Sam was ruining his life.

Sam had long abandoned his yearning for his father's approval. On the rare occasions when they did things together, Sam remembered only criticism when he did things differently than his dad expected. He was certain that his dad loved him in his own way, but he had no recollections of playing ball or other games with him, nor did he remember any close physical contact. Sam did not think his father felt pride in him, especially now.

So instead Sam learned at an early age to seek praise and the companionship of older men among teachers, coaches, and friends' fathers. He had learned to ignore his father's disapproval, and he still tried to avoid the man's anger, which could be intense at times. Therefore, Sam was not exactly surprised by the disapproval from his dad when he resigned. In fact, he expected it. But he was shaken by his dad's vehemence over it and angry at his father's refusal to even entertain the notion that Sam's concerns could be valid.

Right after Sam resigned, his father had arranged for him to meet a family friend named Dale. Dale flew as a navigator with his dad in World War II and was now a college psychology professor at the University of Denver. Sam knew Dale growing up and had liked him immensely. He always radiated optimism and humor. On his father's arrangement, Sam got a day pass to visit Dale and his wife, Emily.

Dale took Sam to his den, which was paneled in dark wood with a crackling fire in a stone fireplace on one wall that was surrounded by bookshelves. A desk faced a window on an adjacent side of the room. Dale directed Sam to sit in one stuffed chair against the opposite wall while Dale sat in a matching chair nearby. Dale had poured them both drinks. Sam found out eventually that one of Dale's most effective psychological methods was to ply his patient with scotch while he secretly watered down his own drinks and kept his head. While not perhaps an approved psychological treatment, it worked with Sam. Emily floated in and out of the den, bringing their drinks and small sandwiches with the crusts cut off. She surely had to be an accomplice in the drink deception.

Up front, Dale informed him that his father had begged him to try to convince Sam to remain at the academy. Dale had declined to do so. He had instead agreed that they would just talk and try to see if they could figure out what was in Sam's head.

"Why is Dad so hostile about me changing my mind?" asked Sam.

"That's a good question. It may have something to do with a theory of mine. I think that adolescence and teenage-hood are biological traits first developed by our ancient ancestors. They were nature's way of making sure you got kicked out of the cave when it was the right time, so to speak," he chuckled. "But seriously, I have known your dad for many years, and he is one of my best friends. We're quite different, though, and took quite different paths. I left the air force after the war. I couldn't wait to get out. But your dad made a career of it. Maybe he feels like you are questioning his own choices." Dale paused and pulled on his pipe. "I don't think there's just one reason for his anger. Let's face it—he grew up as the oldest child, so he led his other siblings. Then the military taught him that with rank, you can expect unquestioned obedience. As captain and commander of our plane during the war, he was practically a god in his mid-twenties. The crew, including me, worshipped him for saving our asses many times. Flying a plane in combat left no room for questions or deviant behavior from any of the crew. He was in sole control on missions.

"Then he comes home. He believes that, as head of the family, he still has the rank and the right. But you come along, bucking that authority. You have different values than he does. If you were someone else, that would be OK. But you're his son, and that threatens him as a father. I'll bet he feels like he should throw you in the brig sometimes, huh?"

"That sounds accurate," said Sam. "But I'm pretty sick of it."

"It may help you to realize that even though he has a strange way of showing it, he loves you intensely. This just happens to be how he shows his love because that is how his life has told him to act," Dale said with a pointed look, taking a sip.

"Lucky me," said Sam.

"Think about it. Would you rather have a father who ignores you and really doesn't give a damn what you do?"

"Let me think about that a minute," Sam said, but he smiled.

Dale laughed and raised his fake drink to toast. They both sipped their scotches and thought in silence.

Dale said, "The important thing to remember is that it may not even be about you. He may be reacting to other stresses in his life. Life can be challenging when you start as a god in your mid-twenties. How do you follow that up?"

They spent the rest of the day exploring a variety of subjects, playing catch-up since the time they had last seen one another. Sam was having a wonderful time during their conversations. Dale was funny and wise, and he had already been able to provide Sam with some insights about his dad, helping him to understand his father's motivations and actions in ways Sam hadn't previously considered. Sam also found that through this, he was finding more of himself than he ever thought existed.

Dale finally circled back to the topic Sam knew was the reasoning for their meetup. When he did, he got straight to the point. "So why do you want to leave the academy?"

Sam blathered on about changes in career plans, lack of motivation, and unjust wars. Dale listened patiently while sipping on his pretend drink and puffing on his pipe.

"OK," Dale said sagely. "Now tell me why you *really* want to leave the academy."

And on it went. Sam was tired of trying to explain what he himself did not fully understand. But he certainly did try. At the end of it, Dale announced, "Let's see if I've got this straight: Young men go to military schools and monasteries because they want to change themselves. But you're pretty much OK with the way you already are, or at least OK with what you're heading to be."

The clouds opened up.

"Bingo!" Sam said.

Dale, true to his psychological skills, had uncovered one of Sam's primary fears and reasons for leaving. Not only did Sam not want the academy to change him, but he was scared, almost to the point of panic, of the personality changes he was already seeing in himself. Did his dad become cold and distant because of his war experiences and military career? Sam was determined not to go down that path.

On the other hand, Dale had gently nudged him to believe that his dad was doing the best he could. Sam knew his dad loved him. His dad had instilled a love of adventure in Sam by the experiences he provided to Sam and his family. He was a good man who always strove to do the right thing. Although Sam would have preferred more *Leave It to Beaver* moments, he knew he had little to complain about. His dad was acting almost exactly as Sam had expected, but that certainly did not make it any easier.

12 ——————————— April 27, 1969

The next morning, Sam awoke to the rumbling of a semitruck outside his window at the Mountain Vista Motel in Burlington, Colorado. Strong sunlight beamed through the gap in the plaid curtains. He rolled over in bed and tried to close them, but instead felt a sharp pain between his eyes, which stopped him in mid-roll. It took him a moment to realize that he was not shot in the head, only somewhat poisoned by last night's tequila.

He slowly eased off the bed, managing to get to the edge and attain a sitting position. He sat there, trying to stop the sloshing of his brain in his skull. He struggled to bring his watch into focus and saw that it was ten in the morning. He was still fully dressed. He got up and managed to finally close the curtains.

"Water," Sam croaked.

He lurched across the cheap wood-paneled room to the kitchenette sink, making sure the various parts of his body still worked together. The faucet dripped onto the rust-stained sink. He got a glass out of the cabinet and inspected it, concluding it seemed about the only clean thing around. He turned the faucet handle, and in response, it squealed in protest. After a few coughs and sputters, water gushed into the sink. He filled his glass and peered in. The water was slightly brown with small particles floating in it.

"Well, no big chunks anyway," he said.

He sipped the water. He tasted a little dirt and metal, reminding him of the school swing his sister Kay had forced him to lick in the winter when he was a kid. But he thought it beat the hell out of the creek water he drank during academy survival training. He gulped down the whole glass.

He winced as he opened the curtains again. The bright light caused the back of his eyes to ache. He looked across the street and saw a place with a sign that labeled it Rose's Café. It was a white one-story building with picture windows. It looked like they knew how to deep fry stuff, and the parking lot was full.

"Maybe some breakfast will cure me," he said, stretching.

When he walked into Rose's Café, he saw a counter running along one side of the room, in front of the kitchen's serving window. High stools were bolted to the floor in front of the counter, padded with pastel-blue vinyl. Sam noticed one row of booths against the café's windows and a row of tables in the middle of the room. Against the far wall, a juke box was playing "Harper Valley PTA" by Jeanie C. Riley.

An older woman with bleached blonde hair, wearing a pale-pink waitress dress, stood behind the counter near the door. Her nametag said "Rose." Sam wondered if she was the Rose who owned the cafe. She was rolling up silverware in napkins when she glanced up at Sam. "Sit anywhere you want, hon," she said with a smile.

The café was about half filled with customers. Sam saw five middle-aged men sitting at a large table at the far end, dressed in heavy overalls and wearing baseball caps. All sipped coffee from white porcelain cups while three of them smoked cigarettes. The remains of the men's breakfasts lay upon their plates. They were all large men weathered by the prairie sun and wind, and they talked and laughed in the easy way of close friends meeting for their ten-thousandth breakfast at Rose's.

"Hey, Robert," one of the men shouted to his buddy. "Where's Billy these days? He too good to meet us for breakfast anymore?"

"Ya know Billy and that widow Doris are playing house now," answered Robert. "I hear he's getting some home cookin' these days."

They all chuckled. After sipping their coffee and blowing smoke into the air, the farmers continued to discuss the weather, the price of seed and fertilizer, and their hopes for their crops they were just now planting in the ground.

Sam took one of the booths near the windows. A black-haired waitress who looked to be in her forties came to his table. Her nametag read "Gloria." She flashed a genuine smile and said, "You look like you could use a decent meal, honey. Need some coffee?"

"Like life itself," he said. "Thank you."

"Comin' right up. Here's a menu."

He opened it after she handed it to him. Although the tequila was still affecting his appetite, he was determined to fuel up for whatever lay ahead. When Gloria returned to the table with his coffee, he ordered three scrambled eggs, bacon, sausage, hash browns, and toast. He ordered the hash browns covered with chopped onions and cheese.

"Good boy!" said Gloria.

He stared out the window at the semis and pickup trucks rolling past the café. He listened to the conversations around him, the clattering of dishes in the kitchen, and Jeanie C. Riley lamenting about social inequity on the jukebox. He relaxed and let his mind go where it wanted to go.

"Order up!" yelled the cook.

Gloria brought his food and refilled his coffee cup.

Sam sipped his coffee and bit into his bacon. *Perfect*, he thought. Just crisp enough but not overcooked. The salty taste complemented the eggs, which were light and fluffy. The hash browns were fried to a crunch on the outside while still tender on the inside—just the way Sam liked them.

His appetite had definitely returned. He wolfed his food down for a few minutes and then settled down to a more civilized pace. When he was done, there was nothing left but a half-eaten hash brown that he could not bring himself to finish.

He heard someone slipping into his own booth across the table from him. Surprised, Sam looked up to see an ancient man in a brown cowboy hat facing him. He wore thick-rimmed glasses, which enlarged his eyes. He was skinny and frail, made more apparent by his clothes, which were too large for him. The man's wrinkled face further contorted into a wide grin, showing yellowed teeth.

"Can I do anything for you, sir?" asked Sam.

"Oh no, young fella. I was just over there," he said, nodding across the room, "and saw ya by yourself over here. Ya seemed like somebody I'd like to know. I can see ya ain't from Burlington. I know everybody in this town. Been here all my life. My name is Andy."

Sam put his coffee cup down and held out his hand. They shook. "Glad to meet you. I'm Sam."

Andy took off his glasses. He reached over, took one of Sam's napkins, and started cleaning the glasses with it. "Yep, nothin' happens here I don't know about," he said. He looked around the room. "Take that sweet lookin' lady over there," he said, motioning his head toward a very large woman sitting at a nearby table. "Alice's no-count husband left her a year ago for the checkout girl at Patterson Grocery. Alice was left with a wet-nosed kid in diapers on her hip. She deserves better than that."

Sam sipped his coffee. "So . . . what? You wanting to rescue Alice from her troubles or something?"

Andy slapped the table and chuckled. "Do I look like I can rescue anybody? Anyway, Alice took him to the woodshed in the divorce, so maybe she can rescue me." He chuckled and put Sam's napkin in his shirt pocket as he seemed to wistfully think about that possibility. "But enough about me. Whataya doin' here, Sam?"

"I'm heading east. Just needed a bite to eat first."

"Sorry to see you go. We could use a young, strappin' guy like yourself 'round here. Now, I understand how you might think there's nothin' around here for a guy like you. But I like it. It's my home. I struggle some at times but wouldn't change a thing." He paused. "Well, maybe I'd like the change to a rich girlfriend."

They laughed. Sam found his company easy.

"You hang out at Rose's a lot?" asked Sam.

"Oh, ya. Ya want to meet women in Burlington, ya come to Rose's."

Sam looked around the room at the girlfriend prospects and smiled. He thought about people's differing tastes.

Gloria came to the table with a coffee pot.

"Now, Andy, what've I told ya 'bout botherin' the customers? Let the poor boy eat his breakfast without havin' to listen to your nonsense."

"My darlin', I *am* a customer. In fact, I'll treat *you* to lunch—right here, right now," he said as he patted the seat next to him. "If you'll have me."

"Why, aren't *you* the big spender! This place is rated five stars, I hear. Best cuisine in the West. But I'll bet you'd forget your wallet and make me pay for it."

Andy leered at Gloria. She laughed, shook her head, and walked away. Andy reached across the table. "Ya done with those hash browns?"

Sam walked out of the café with more power than he entered with. At least his legs were steady and working right, and he certainly felt better. If Andy could be optimistic about meeting women, maybe Sam could be optimistic about things too.

He walked back to his room to recover his bag and dragged it across the motel parking lot to the side of the road. Sam surveyed his surroundings. Some things were different from when darkness had descended last night. He was on the edge of the town, and he looked away toward an unbroken horizon under a leaden, overcast sky.

Sam stood on Rose Avenue, almost a mile from Interstate 70, knowing it was not a great place to hitchhike. He needed to get to the highway. Luckily, Sam had to admit that the Air Force Academy had really toughened him up and caused him to be in pretty great shape due to their constant orders to run. At least he was strong and could easily make his way across impressive distances for it. Sam found himself to be grateful for this now as he spent what seemed like forever dragging his bag as far as he could, pausing to catch his breath, then repeating the task.

Beyond being required to run everywhere all year, it was during boot camp that freshmen cadets really had to run. Boot camp, by definition, was constant exercise runs, punishment runs, runs wearing this, runs wearing that, etc. A grunt did not walk anywhere. Failure to run properly caused upperclassmen to descend on a poor grunt like vultures.

The obstacle course was especially grim and was certainly designed by the Marquis de Sade. It was a tenuous race over rough ground strewn with torturous obstacles like tangled barbed wire to crawl under, walls to climb over, mud to slither through, ropes to swing over gullies, and water hazards to crash through like steeplechase horses. When Sam ran the course, every one of his muscles was so exhausted by the end that he could barely control himself. Luckily other cadets lined up at the finish line and caught him. They even walked him around to keep his muscles from cramping up. Not everyone was so fortunate. Sam heard of one cadet who'd had a heart attack and died right there on the course.

A freshman cadet was also subject, at any time, to a variety of very imaginative, if not sadistic, rituals. These included dropping for pushups, sweating for your shower, and the Imaginary Chair. Sam could do a lot of pushups and had a talent for sweating, but he dreaded being subjected to the Imaginary Chair. It involved sitting on nothing with his back to the wall and ass hanging in the air, trying to hold that position until he collapsed in a pile on the floor. Some cruel upperclassmen added the holding of an M1 rifle out in front with outstretched arms. Sam could not hold it for long before he lost control of his own.

During boot camp, Sam's group of fifteen—called a flight—was running in formation on a gravel road at the back of the academy. They wore green fatigues and black combat boots. One upperclassman ran alongside the formation and barked out the cadence while another took up the rear.

Sam's flight leader during boot camp, a senior named Patrick, sometimes led the runs. Patrick was the quarterback of the AFA Falcons football team. In addition to calling out the cadence, Patrick would shout out encouragement and some philosophy. When a run became long and the cadets were faltering, he yelled, "Don't just look down at the ground. Look around you at this amazing scenery. People pay big money to come to Colorado and enjoy these surroundings. Don't focus on your pain. Focus on what you see. Breathe in the sweet air."

One of Sam's mates was a large, beefy guy from Waco, Texas, named Marty Walker. Marty was an impressive sprinter with a hundred-yard-dash time of ten seconds flat. But after two hundred yards on a long-distance run, Marty would begin to fail.

On that particular morning, Marty was on the outside of the formation and started to stumble along, dragging his feet, his eyes rolling back in his head. The two upperclassmen closed in on Marty like sharks, running next to him. They got in his face.

"Ya big pussy!" one shouted. "Ya shoulda told us your legs didn't work when ya joined up."

"Now you're holding everybody back!" shouted the other.

His mates around him, in the spirit of leaving no man behind, ran beside Marty and tried to prop him up. He struggled on, his face turning red and his stumbling worsening. Other cadets stepped in as those holding up Marty faltered. Finally, he lurched sideways from the formation and weaved to the side of the road, crashing to the ground. One of the upperclassmen stopped and continued shouting at Marty while he lay there on the side of the road, the rest of the flight thundering on.

The next morning, they assembled for their run as usual.

"Now we don't want you to get hurt, Cadet Walker," one upperclassman said. "So one of your mates will carry a pillow so you won't get all scratched up this time." The other upperclassman gave a pillow to the cadet next to Marty.

As Marty stalled and careened off the road this time, the other cadet with the pillow followed him and tried to toss it under him before he collapsed. One upperclassman stopped again to scream at Marty about his shortcomings.

Marty was a very tough person and tried to hang in there, especially after being singled out for humiliation. But his body was just not designed to be a long-distance runner. A week later after no improvement in Marty's performance, the flight was gathered at attention again before their run.

One upperclassman stood beside a chair. "I've got to tell ya, my friend and I are wearing ourselves out standing near Cadet Walker and urging him to soldier on. So, in addition to the pillow, two more of you will carry this chair so that neither my friend nor I have to stand around while we're waiting for your fellow cadet to rise again."

For a few more weeks, the flight continued to run in the morning with the pillow and chair. They became very skilled at passing them around so that everyone shared the load. After those few weeks, the upperclassmen grew bored with that torture and moved on to other diabolical schemes.

Marty somehow survived boot camp.

All these physical demands were, of course, scientifically designed by the air force to produce lean, mean, fighting machines. While Sam did not totally agree with this goal or their methods, he did have to admit that it got him in top shape. Sam felt able to deal with almost anything as a result—that was physical, at least.

13 ——————————— April 27, 1969

Sam finished dragging his bag to a better location. He stood on the entrance ramp to Interstate 70. Sam saw three solo male hitchhikers and a young couple scattered along the ramp and highway merge lane, spaced out so drivers could see they were not riding together. Sam positioned himself closest to the highway, taking his turn in line behind the couple. It was noon, but the low overcast and wind sucked most of the warmth out of the air. Traffic on I-70 was much heavier than the traffic he encountered on the two-lane road last night. The three men were picked up quickly.

A Dodge Charger finally rolled by Sam and pulled over. Sam quickly dragged his bag to the car. He opened the wide passenger door, pulled the back of the front bucket seat forward, hefted his bag onto the back seat, and jumped in.

The driver was dressed in a starched white shirt and tie, his checkered sport coat draped over the seat back. He appeared to Sam to be about fifty years old but in good shape. His hair was cut in a crew cut on top of his bullet-like head. There was a ridge on top of his skull, which being closer to the top of his crew cut, appeared like a mountain ridge just above the clouds. He wore black glasses and was clean-shaven. Frank Sinatra crooned "My Way" on the radio as the driver moved his sport coat to the back seat.

Sam reached out his hand to shake, then said, "Hi, I'm Sam."

"Leonard," the driver curtly answered. He raised his hand in a half salute. After a few seconds, Sam withdrew his hand and half saluted back.

"Where ya goin', sport?" asked Leonard as he pulled away.

"St. Louis, sir," answered Sam.

"Well, this is your lucky day," said Leonard. "That's where I'm going too. You live there?"

"I've been in St. Louis since I was eleven years old. I'm an air force brat and was all over the place before that."

"How'd you like all that moving around?"

"I loved it, but I think my sisters hated it. It was always a big adventure to me. I'm glad I was in one place since I was eleven, though. Having long-term friends through your teenage years was great. My sisters were not so lucky and were moved all around when one was in high school, and the other was in junior high. They had trouble making new friends."

"Born and bred in St. Louis, myself," said Leonard.

The Charger rolled down I-70. Leonard stared out the front window in silence.

Sam tried to think of conversation starters. He remembered that when two people from St. Louis met, the first thing each asked was where they went to high school. Sam thought Leonard might be too old to play that game, so he searched his mind for another ice breaker.

"You a Cardinal fan, Leonard?"

"Baseball or football Cardinals?" asked Leonard.

"I guess either . . . or both."

Leonard thought a minute. "No, not really," he finally said.

Oh, the strong silent type, thought Sam. *So much for sports small talk.*

They rode on in awkward silence. Sam started to ask Leonard where he went to high school just for the hell of it, but stopped at the last second. "You also work in St. Louis?" he decided to ask instead.

Leonard again paused. "Yeah, I do."

Again, silence.

Sam gave up trying to start a conversation. He stared out the side window.

After an excruciating silence, Leonard finally asked, "You a student?"

"Not right now, sir. I'm looking to get enrolled at another college."

Leonard looked Sam up and down, his eyes narrowing below his furrowed brow. "If you don't mind me saying, you don't look like a student to me. Those shiny combat boots and your haircut say 'military' to me. I would know. I served in Europe in World War II."

Sam had no intention to recite his history to Leonard. He could not envision this man to be the sympathetic type, especially not with Sam's story.

"So, what's your deal?" asked Leonard. "You a deserter or something?"

Sam reluctantly decided to tell the truth. "No, I was just discharged from the Air Force Academy."

"They kick you out?" Leonard asked.

"No, sir. I resigned."

"You resigned?" Leonard's face flushed as he gripped the steering wheel. Sam was starting to hope he might just be able to leave it with a replied, "Yes, sir." But instead Leonard continued, his voice angry and louder than it had been before. "What kinda ungrateful shit are you?"

"Now hold on." Sam tried to sound reasonable and calm, but he could feel his own anger building as well.

"Hold on, my ass!" Leonard shouted. "I was honored to serve under Patton in the war. It wasn't easy, but we liberated Europe. I would've given my left nut to get the chance to be an officer."

Sam said, "I can understand that, sir, and I really do respect your service."

"Don't give me that shit! You think you're too good to serve your country when it calls?"

"No, sir, I don't feel I'm too good, but I just don't see the point if that service is in Vietnam. I don't believe we need to be fighting there."

"You don't get to choose where and when to fight, you nitwit. You do what your country needs you to do."

Sam said, "Believe it or not, I do get it. You fought for our rights and freedoms in World War II. That's wonderful, and I admire you for that.

But with the fighting in Vietnam, it's just not the same. Our rights and freedoms aren't affected by Vietnam in that same way, so I don't see why I should give up my rights, my freedoms, and maybe even my life to fight there, that's all."

"Bullshit! With you people, it will take the communists taking over your hometown before you realize the threat. You and your commie friends only care about smoking dope and feeling up your hippie chicks."

Sam felt his face warm in resentment. "Respectfully, sir, I disagree," he managed to get out in as level of a voice as he could muster. Internally, he wanted to punch the man. Sam was again hoping the conversation would simply end there and found himself missing the awkward silence.

"Bullshit," Leonard spat back.

"Alright, whatever," Sam finally muttered dismissively, realizing now that the civil approach wasn't doing either of them any favors.

Leonard hit the brakes hard. Sam just managed to cover his face with his arms before he crashed into the metal dashboard. Leonard pulled abruptly to the side of the road and skidded to a stop in the gravel. He turned to Sam and glared.

"'Whatever,' huh?" Leonard spat. His face was red, and veins stood out on his forehead.

"What the fuck is wrong with you?" yelled Sam.

"You know what? You're just a goddamned coward! I want ya the hell out of my car."

"Fine, you son of a bitch," Sam yelled back.

Sam opened the car door. As the door was still open and he was stepping out, Leonard smashed the accelerator and spun off in a hail of gravel. Sam dove to the side as the door slammed shut from the momentum. He rolled once and sprang up again. The Charger stopped about fifty feet away. Leonard got out of the car, reached into the back seat for Sam's bag, and threw it into the ditch next to the road. He got back in the car and took off again.

As the car pulled away, Sam picked up a rock and threw it. It made a satisfying *thunk* against the back of the trunk. He yelled, "Who the fuck you think you are? So sorry about your new paint job, you bastard!"

Leonard stopped the car, and it sat running on the side of the road. The car's white backup lights came on, and the car slowly rolled back toward him. Sam looked around; there was nowhere to hide on the empty plain. Even though Leonard was into late middle age, he still looked powerful enough to do some damage. He wouldn't be surprised if Leonard also had a gun.

Sam ran to his bag, unzipped it, and pulled out the small shovel he had purchased at K-Mart. He raised it as a challenge. The car continued to slowly come at him. He swung the shovel in a circle over his head as the car came closer. He then ran toward it, still swinging the shovel as a warning. He roared like a charging bear.

The car's red brake lights came on. Sam stopped running but kept the shovel high above his head. No one moved for what seemed an eternity. Finally, the car's backup lights went out, then the brake lights. The Dodge rolled slowly away. Leonard eventually pulled the car onto the highway and squealed the tires as he accelerated away.

Sam dropped the shovel and shivered with the excess adrenalin flooding him. After a few moments, it caught up to him what had just happened.

"What a dick!" muttered Sam.

14 ——————————— April 27, 1969

It took fifteen minutes for Sam to calm down. He looked around at where he had been so unceremoniously dumped on the road. About fifty feet ahead, Sam saw a billboard showing a very hairy rodent next to a wooly mammoth and a saber-toothed tiger, all surrounded by lush vegetation. "SEE THE LARGEST PRAIRIE DOG THAT EVER LIVED!" shouted the billboard. "RELIVE PREHISTORIC TIMES WHEN GIANT MAMMALS ROAMED THE PLAINS—KANORADO, KANSAS."

Sam's family took many long car trips when he was younger. He and his sisters begged to stop at places like this. But his dad always maintained a strict schedule, making such excursions impossible. There was always somewhere they had to be by dinner. Every move of their vacations was planned in great detail, depicted on AAA roadmaps. They sped by reptile farms, caverns, Native American museums, and other roadside attractions while trying to not think about how badly they had to pee. His sister Kay tried to tickle him into losing control of his bladder, and his parents always played bland orchestral music on the radio, which all sounded the same. Unscheduled stops were denied, only until Sam's mom insisted.

"Now that's something I need to see," said Sam to himself, gazing at the billboard.

Just then a dirty, semi-white Ford truck slowed down to check him out, pulling to the side of the road just past Sam.

At almost a run, Sam dragged his bag forward to the truck and threw it into the truck bed in one continuous motion. His bag-wrangling moves were improving. There was a saddle, coiled ropes, and a variety of muddy tools in the truck bed, along with a large black-and-white dog who barked a friendly greeting and then grinned. His brown eyes looked almost human. The dog did not rush to him to be petted but instead regarded Sam with a friendly but professional air. The dog came toward him and smelled his hands, then grinned again.

Sam glanced through the truck's partially open back window and saw a large, white cowboy hat on the driver's head, which kept Sam from seeing much more of him. Sam opened the passenger side door, lifted himself up to the bench seat, and closed the door.

The cowboy looked to be in his late twenties or early thirties. His blue eyes were surrounded by fine lines, likely caused by sun, wind, and a sense of humor. The cowboy smiled and threw out his hand. "Hey, buddy. How ya doin'?"

"I'm doing fine. Thanks for picking me up. My name's Sam."

"Glad to meet ya, Sam. I'm Travis."

They shook hands. Travis's grip was strong, and his hands were thickly calloused.

Travis pushed the clutch pedal to the floor, shifted the steering-column stick into first gear, and released the clutch while smoothly accelerating. The truck rolled through the gravel back onto the entrance ramp. Travis was dressed in a red-and-black western-style shirt with pearl snaps. He had on jeans and worn-out cowboy boots. The inside of his truck reflected hard work outdoors: covered in dust while also littered with food wrappers and empty beer cans.

"See ya passed the test with Blackie back there," Travis said. "He's usually a good judge of character."

"Great lookin' dog," said Sam. "Looks smart as hell too."

"Oh, he's scary smart all right. You might call him a deep thinker. He's some kind of German shepherd-collie mix. He thinks he's in charge, and I don't usually argue with him about it."

Sam looked through the back window at Blackie staring back at him. He was still grinning and was shifting his attention from Sam to Travis as each spoke like he understood what they were saying perfectly.

"Blackie likes to go to town, sometimes to find me when I'm there, and sometimes just 'cause he wants to. One time he came into a bank while I was tryin' to get a loan and found me in the bank manager's office. Boy, was he ever proud of himself that day!"

"How far from town are you?" asked Sam. "Seems like a long way for Blackie to walk."

"Oh, we're thirty-five miles south of Kanorado. But Blackie doesn't walk, he hitchhikes."

"What?" Sam asked, making sure he heard him right.

"He stands out on the road and gets in front of any truck or car he knows until they stop. Then he jumps in and rides to town. When he's ready to come back, he finds a parked car or truck he knows and waits for them to show up. If it's a truck, he just jumps up into the truck bed and takes a nap."

Sam looked back at Blackie. This time Blackie looked away, avoiding further scrutiny. He barked at a passing cow instead.

"I think he has a girlfriend in town," Travis continued. "I saw him once with a small collie, lickin' melted ice cream off the sidewalk in front of Rexall's."

"Sounds like a date to me," said Sam.

They rode in silence for a few minutes. This time around, it was comfortable.

"How far ya goin'?" asked Travis.

"Eventually I want to get to St. Louis," answered Sam.

"Whoa, that's a ways! I'm only goin' just over the border myself. We got a small cattle ranch there."

"I kinda thought you might be a cowboy," Sam said, gesturing toward the truck bed carrying saddles, ropes, and other cowboy gear.

"You must be a college guy to get those powers of deduction," Travis said. His tone was deadpan, but his happy eyes and slight smile showed he was kidding.

"Yeah, I guess you could call me that." said Sam. "I'm just between colleges right now." He paused for a few seconds. "I've heard that cowboying is an exciting life," he said. "Full of riding and roping, sleeping under the open skies, being one with nature and the herd and all that—"

Travis snorted. "And freezing your ass off in the cold rain, smellin' cow farts all day, and only talkin' to your horse."

They both laughed.

Travis's face turned serious. "I love the life, though. I've been runnin' the ranch since my dad died five years ago. It's where I grew up, and we're raising a family here. I have a good wife and two boys who run wild all over it. Someday it'll all be theirs." Travis gazed out the dirty windshield and tapped the steering wheel. "But it's gettin' harder and harder to make ends meet. I'm afraid a family ranch means worry . . . and workin' long, hard hours all day, all month, and all year. Even then, we're lucky to break even when it's all done."

"Sorry to hear that," said Sam. He struggled to respond further. "What's causing all of it?"

"Cattle prices are in the dirt right now, hardly covering our costs. It's hard to compete against the big outfits. They can cut their costs per head by spreadin' the costs across more cattle, and they can afford things I can't, just because they're big."

"You seem to know a lot about the ranching business, though," said Sam.

"Yah, like that helps." But the twinkle had returned to Travis's eyes, seemingly taking pride in this. He paused. "No, I'm kidding. I'm sure knowing what you're doin' does actually help. But the best plan in the world looks pretty stupid after a hailstorm kills your cows, or it doesn't rain for three months, or a tornado knocks down your barn." He paused again. "I'd have to say, though, that it all becomes worth it when we live and work for ourselves in this beautiful place. Continuing that, any way I can, is my goal. We may never be rich, but that's not the point."

Sam looked out the window at the flat plain flowing past them. It was a tan and brown world, featureless across the empty expanse. He thought that maybe it's the love of the homeland that makes it beautiful to someone.

"Blackie sure helps out around the place," Travis said. "Don't you, boy?" he shouted toward the back window.

Blackie barked twice. It sounded like he said, "Sure do."

"Actually," said Travis in a lower, confidential voice as he moved his head closer to Sam, "Blackie is sorta a fair-weather cow-dog. He's out with me and the herd most days when the weather is nice, but a snow, hailstorm, or big rain will find him in a bed at the ranch, under the covers."

Sam grinned. "Sounds like he's got things pretty well figured out." He watched the road for several minutes. "Is it just you, your wife, and your two boys here?" he finally asked.

"For now. My kid brother, Jesse, is in Vietnam and will be coming back later this year. I need to figure how he can jump back in. He does have a piece of the operation, but the ranch is really too small to split up. Being the oldest, it was pretty much understood that I would run things." He stopped for a moment. "I guess that's a big part of why Jesse enlisted in the army. He saw a purpose in it and a way to get the training he needed to have more options. And, you know, I don't think he regrets it."

Sam felt a twinge of uncomfortableness at the topic that had ended so poorly for him on his last ride. But he also knew Travis was about as far different from Leonard than two people could get. "How's Vietnam been for him?" Sam asked finally.

"He feels like he's done some good over there," Travis answered easily. "Jesse has experienced some bad shit, and he tells me that few have been angels over there. But he believes he's helped defend his platoon brothers and Vietnamese villagers against the Vietcong, who have been pretty much ruthless with anyone who opposes them."

Sam thought in silence. He fully understood Jesse's dedication and recognized the pride in Travis's voice when he spoke of his brother. The last thing he wanted to do was blather on about his resistance to the war. Sam decided how to respond. "I admire your brother's service," he said. And that was that.

The truck approached a billboard. As it got closer, Sam saw that it was another LARGEST PRAIRIE DOG sign. Sam pointed to the sign and asked, "That worth seein', Travis?"

"Oh, the prairie dog?" Travis paused. "I wouldn't miss it if I were you. It's one of our most famous attractions, and people come from far and wide to see it. I think it's a real interesting place."

"I'll take you up on that then."

"I'd drop you off right there, Sam, but I have to be at my place for an appointment. I can get you pretty close, though."

"Thanks, Travis. I'd appreciate that."

Fifteen minutes later they saw the exit sign for Kanorado, followed quickly by a sign stating, LEAVING COLORFUL COLORADO. Sam could see the town in the distance north of the interstate. He saw small homes and buildings nestled among trees, forming a prairie oasis. Sam thought the trees were probably planted by the town's settlers, likely to help block the wind and relieve the monotony of the flat surroundings. He saw a huge cluster of grain elevators dominating the horizon on the east side of the town. The town was behind them in seconds.

Another exit sign appeared for County Road 3.

"This's where I have to turn south," said Travis as he turned on his blinker. "If you go north on three about a mile to old US-24, you'll find the place. Believe me, you'll love it."

Travis turned right onto the exit, and they drove down to the end of the ramp. He pulled the truck over to the side of County Road 3. They reached across the front seat and shook hands.

"Thanks again for the ride, Travis," said Sam. "It was good meeting you, and I hope you have the best of luck with your ranch."

"Likewise." Travis pumped Sam's hand. "Good luck, Sam. I hope your trip to St. Louis goes well."

Sam climbed out of the truck and pulled his bag out of the truck bed. Blackie barked goodbye.

"Bye, Blackie. Nice to meet you."

Blackie barked in what seemed to be a "You too."

He raised his right hand toward Travis. Travis raised his left arm out the window as he was driving off.

Sam listened to the truck run through its gears and remained still as the sound of the truck diminished. He turned his attention north under the interstate overpass and up County Road 3. The land was bare, and the overpass—from Sam's perspective—appeared to loom high above him. The sign pointing back to Kanorado rattled in the wind. He pulled his hood over his head.

Sam didn't want to drag the bag a mile and then back again. He pulled it to the other side of the road. His bag was his lifeline, containing his clothes and other supplies, but he didn't think he had packed anything of super great importance. Any thief would get pretty tired of lugging that bag around anyway. He opened a side pocket, removed a roll of bills, and put the roll in his inside coat pocket. He looked around for a hiding place. Sam could not see a tree anywhere or even any grass high enough to hide it.

"I guess I could bury it," he said to himself.

Instead, he saw a piece of warped broken plywood laying in a fallow field. He pulled the bag over to it, lifted the plywood and kicked the bag under it. He leaned the plywood over it to block any view of it.

He walked up the road, feeling light and mobile without the additional weight. He soon broke into an easy jog. Once he reached the other side of the highway overpass, he saw a small sign on a stake driven into the ground. FEEL THE THRILL, read the sign. Sam jogged about a hundred yards more and saw another sign reading, LIVE THE HISTORY. In another hundred yards, he read, SEE THE WORLD'S LARGEST PRAIRIE DOG IN ONE MILE.

He covered the mile easily before approaching an intersection for US-24. County Road 3 turned to gravel on the other side. A metal windowless building was a few hundred feet away. The front wall of it was a faded green-and-brown mural showing the prairie dog with wooly mammoths, giant sloths, and other extinct creatures in the background. The mural was painted over a door with a sign on it that read, ADMISSION: TWENTY-FIVE CENTS, KIDS FREE.

Sam opened the door. In the dim light he could see a small room with tropical plants made of plaster and plastic. The walls were painted in camouflage. In the corner, a stuffed mountain lion was frozen in mid-snarl, claws brandished against the tourists. It appeared a taxidermist had grafted two large, curved fangs into the mountain lion's mouth which extended far beneath his jaw.

Sam was studying the "saber-toothed" mountain lion when there was a movement in the dim corner to the left of Sam's vision. Startled, he jerked his head and saw a small man standing behind a counter. The man could have been any age from forty to sixty. He was slightly built, completely bald, and wore round wire-rim glasses.

"Wanna go in?" the man asked, without any appearance of caring whether Sam's answer was yes or no.

"Uh, I guess so," answered Sam. He handed the man a quarter from his pocket.

The man pointed to another metal door also painted in camouflage. "Go right through that door."

Sam pushed the door open into another dim hall. The walls were painted with jungle foliage. The hall was a maze with blocked passageways, mirrors, and unexpected entrances further in. After several bumps and turns, he stumbled across another jungle-painted door. He opened it.

In the middle of a large room, he saw a fat, brown figure that stood about twelve feet tall. Sam walked slowly around it. He felt it and found it was made of concrete. The workmanship made it hard to tell what kind of animal it was. He thought it could have been a prairie dog, but it also could have been a gopher, groundhog, beaver, or even a bear.

Sam saw no signs or plaques explaining what it was or why anyone would make such a thing. He scratched his head. "Good one, Travis," he muttered. "How many times have you pulled that one?" He figured at least that Travis was probably having a good laugh about it.

15 —————————— April 27, 1969

Sam jogged back from the "museum." He recovered his bag from the field and was standing on the I-70 entrance ramp just outside Kanorado, Kansas. He felt a little embarrassed by being totally snookered by Travis but had to give him credit for selling the joke. He was sure Travis would tell the story over the coming years of the gullible hitchhiker he had sent on a wild goose chase, or rather a wild prairie dog chase.

He stood alone on the entrance ramp. He felt the temperature drop as the wind picked up. Large flakes of wet snow began to fall and blow around, driven at a forty-five-degree angle by the wind, pelting him harshly in the face. Traffic had slowed down. It was dusk, and with the snow, Sam could see nothing past fifty feet. Beyond that, there was only an undefined gray mass dominating the sky blocking any further horizons.

"It sure looks like Mother Nature is seriously trying to kill me," he said to himself.

He looked around for some shelter. He saw nothing but bare dirt, now being splotched with clumps of wet snow. He thought about taking refuge under the I-70 overpass at the base of the entrance ramp, but the wind-driven snow was now piling up under that too. There was no shelter from the wind, which was filling the air with the stinging, wet flakes. He searched for anything that might help.

During basic training, cadets spent a week on survival training somewhere in the mountains behind the Air Force Academy. This training was to harden the cadets and help prepare them to be shot down behind enemy lines. Every cadet wanted to be a pilot and most likely pictured himself cruising and owning the skies by day, hanging out at the Officer's Club by night. But getting shot down behind enemy lines was a real terror they all shared.

Sam's fifteen-man group was up at an elevation above the tree line with nothing more than matches, pocketknives, trenching tools, canteens, ponchos, and some rope. Other groups were scattered over the mountains. A cold rain fell on them, and the wind bit at any exposed skin. Sam wished it would get just a little colder and snow. Then they would at least be drier and not slogging through wet mud. There was no shelter, and the cadets huddled on the ground underneath their ponchos to shield themselves.

They had, however, received some training from their upper-class leader at the beginning of the exercise. He showed them some plants they could eat and told them that the best approach to surviving in the wild was to build a shelter and hunker down, conserving energy and calories. Contrary to that advice, Sam and his mates were made to roam over the mountains on a pointless odyssey; hiking about ten miles a day in steep, rugged terrain; gnawing on some roots; and becoming increasingly hungrier and weaker by the minute. Sam dreamt about food as he fitfully tried to sleep under his poncho at night.

They spent five days wandering in the wilderness. The upperclassmen gave them objectives to reach each day and then left them pretty much alone to puzzle over their maps and slosh over the mountains. Sam suspected the upperclassmen were over the next ridge, hanging out in a proper tent with a campfire nearby, feeding on hot cans of rations and s'mores.

The most terrifying night Sam spent was during a thunderstorm. At an elevation near ten thousand feet, they were actually surrounded by the clouds that the lightning flashed through, each one momentarily blazing around them. Sam crawled on his belly to avoid being a lightning rod and hid in a shallow depression. He curled up in a ball and waited to be struck with the next bolt. Sam heard later that one cadet only a short distance away from his group had been killed by a direct lightning strike.

At one point, hunger drove all fifteen of them to chase down a porcupine in some prehistoric tribal hunt, raining rocks on the poor creature until it was dead. They celebrated like their primitive ancestors, dancing around their kill.

However, no one had ever eaten porcupine or knew how to cook it. Nor did anyone know how to remove the porcupine's quills. Someone suggested boiling it. They could build a fire, but where in the hell would they get enough water? Or a pot to hold it and the porcupine? So they tried to singe the porcupine over a hastily built fire, fueled by wood they had hiked down to the tree line to retrieve. The wood was barely dry enough to burn. The porcupine was thrown on top of the smoldering fire. Forty-five minutes later, only a few of the quills had loosened up enough to be removed. Meanwhile, the porcupine became a mangled, bloody mess in the process.

One cadet took a bite and gagged. Several more tried to, but even their driving hunger could not keep the porcupine flesh down. In the end, they gave up and buried the porcupine, placing some rocks over the hastily made grave.

One cadet stepped forward and placed his hand over his heart. "We thank you, Mr. Porcupine," he said. "We thank you for giving your life to sustain us in this wilderness. And we thank you for pointing out that we don't know shit about surviving out here."

Sam lost another ten pounds and came down with mononucleosis. It struck him after survival training when he was a dinner guest with an officer's family. Grunts were sometimes invited to such dinners to experience family life and help build morale. Sam was weak and pale as he tried to pick over the pork chops, mashed potatoes, and green beans.

He was between bites when he suddenly passed out, slumping face forward into his mashed potatoes.

The officer and his wife took Sam directly to the hospital. He was there for a week, aching like never before and sleeping as much as he could to relieve the weariness. After he was released and back in his quarters, he was berated by upperclassmen for "getting sick out of his chain of command." Their arbitrary judgement added another stone to his wall of resentment against the military for intruding into every aspect of his life. But he at least knew he had picked up some survival skills from the training, if nothing more than learning how shitty things could get but how they could still be survived.

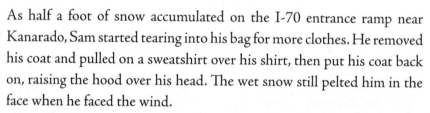

As half a foot of snow accumulated on the I-70 entrance ramp near Kanarado, Sam started tearing into his bag for more clothes. He removed his coat and pulled on a sweatshirt over his shirt, then put his coat back on, raising the hood over his head. The wet snow still pelted him in the face when he faced the wind.

A black Lincoln Continental suddenly rolled into view out of the gray nothingness. It rolled down the highway and approached the end of the entrance ramp where Sam was standing. He heard the clanking of snow chains on the Lincoln's back tires, somewhat muffled by the deepening snow. The car passed Sam and then turned onto the shoulder.

As he approached the car, Sam heard a pop, and the trunk lid rose into the air. Sam threw in his bag, gently closed the trunk, walked around the car, and opened the door. The warmth rushing out the door was delicious and welcoming. Sam smelled leather and felt like he was entering a fine lodge or men's club.

He sank into the passenger seat, closing the door as "This Guy's in Love With You" by Herb Albert crooned on the stereo radio.

Sam reached out his hand. "Thank you so much for stopping, sir. It was getting sketchy out there. My name is Sam Roberts."

"My name's Carl Gilinsky," the man yelled. Sam flinched a little at Carl's loud voice.

Carl was a large, heavy man around fifty. He wore a black-and-white, fine-striped, long-sleeved shirt with a red string tie, held together with a silver ring. He wore black dress pants with shiny black cowboy boots. His friendly blue eyes were set wide apart over his nose and his straight, light-brown hair was neatly parted.

Carl shouted, "Yeah, Sam, you looked like you were getting pretty deep out there. Glad to help. How far you goin'?"

"I'm going as far as you're going on I-70," Sam shouted back.

Carl tilted his head and looked at Sam inquisitively.

"Why ya shoutin', son?" Carl yelled.

Sam stared in confusion.

"I'm sorry, sir," Sam said in a normal voice. "I thought *you* were talking loudly. I thought you might be hard of hearing."

Carl laughed explosively and slapped the steering wheel.

"Well, if that doesn't take all!" said Carl in a little lower voice. He laughed again. "No, my hearing's fine. I'm an auctioneer, and I yell for a living. Sometimes I have no idea how loud I'm talking."

They both laughed.

"You don't need to call me 'sir,'" Carl said. "I'm not your boss. Carl is fine."

"Thanks, Carl."

They stared out the window as the Lincoln glided easily down the road. Sam was mesmerized by the hypnotic falling snow in the headlights and the rhythm of the windshield wipers. The heavy car confidently blasted through the six inches of snow. He could barely hear the chains in the roomy, well-insulated interior. He felt cozy and safe, almost like he was in Carl's living room.

"Where you coming from?" asked Carl.

"I just left the Air Force Academy." He paused. "I resigned last week. I felt I had . . ."

Carl raised his hand to stop him. "That's all right, son. No need to explain. I understand the need to sometimes change your mind."

Sam settled back in his seat and marveled at how comfortable he was. His eyelids were becoming heavy as a deep, tired relief seeped into his body. The Lincoln's leather seat enveloped him.

16 ——————————— April 27, 1969

Sam woke in the passenger's seat of the Lincoln to Carl gently shaking him. "We're home," he shouted. "Welcome to Oakley, Kansas."

Sam shook his head in bewilderment as he tried to get his bearings. He was expecting to get dropped off on the road somewhere. The wind had abated, and the snow was falling straight down in large, wet flakes. Lit by two outdoor lights high on poles, he saw that Carl's yard was a smooth, deep, trackless snowfield. His driveway and the sidewalk leading to the front of the house were both neatly shoveled, although the snow was starting to pile up again. It was almost two feet deep there in the yard.

Sam looked around, confused. As they walked to the house, Sam heard only the distant hum of traffic, the almost inaudible hiss of falling snow, and the crunch of their footsteps—all muted by the piles of white. The house was a substantial square structure in a flat yard. Large trees surrounded the house, sheltering it from prairie winds. The white house was trimmed in dark green with a large porch stretching across the whole front of it. Lugging his bag aimlessly behind him in the snow, Sam continued to follow Carl up the sidewalk to the front porch.

"Sure glad Edna got the little tractor out to plow the snow," Carl shouted. In a quieter voice, he added, "The little lady is handy to have around sometimes."

"I thought you were going to drop me somewhere on I-70," Sam said, still slightly dazed.

"You looked like you needed the sleep, and I wasn't going to leave you out in this mess. I think any motels that are still open are full now from people getting off the roads. Besides, Edna would kill me if I abandoned you out there."

"Well, thank you, Carl," Sam said sincerely. Truth be told, this was more than he had hoped for.

After stomping their feet on the porch to remove the snow, Carl opened the door and waved his arm toward the inside of the house. "Come on in." They stepped into an entry with old, dark, shining oak floors. Sam saw open archways leading to other rooms and a stairway leading up. A standing lamp and a ceiling light fixture provided soft light to the room.

"You can leave your bag here and follow me," Carl told Sam.

They walked through the furthest archway and entered a large kitchen. It was clean and uncluttered, with shining white cabinets over pale green linoleum counters. At the end of one counter, a middle-aged woman stood wiping the counters. When she saw them, she smiled.

"Look who I brought home, Edna," said Carl. "He was about to be covered head to toe in snow, so I had to stop."

Edna Gilinsky was a large woman with light-brown hair and a wholesome, rosy face. She was dressed in a red bathrobe. Sam thought she had probably just woken up when they had arrived.

"Sam, please meet Edna, the love of my life and the real boss of this household. Edna, this is Sam."

He winked at Sam. A glint of amusement flashed in Edna's eyes.

"You better say that, Carl." Edna crossed the room and enveloped Sam in her ample arms. "Welcome, Sam. It's a happy surprise you've come. I'm glad you can stay with us."

"Thank you so much for letting me into your home, ma'am," Sam said. "You have a very beautiful place."

"You're quite welcome, son. But please don't call me 'ma'am.' I'm not an old lady yet."

"Thank you. You certainly aren't."

She gestured to a dinette table on the other side of the kitchen. "You boys look like you could eat something." She did not wait for an answer. She reached up into a cabinet and pulled down a loaf of white bread. She pulled two small plates from another cabinet and placed them on the counter. Then she went to the refrigerator, pulled a jar of mayonnaise from the door, and brought out a square plastic container. "Why don't you boys go sit down, and I'll bring it to you."

Carl and Sam took their seats at the table.

"That was a doozy of a snowstorm, but I've seen worse," commented Carl.

"Seems like the Lincoln Continental was up to the task," added Sam.

"The Lincoln is a beast," answered Carl. "It may seem like a soft and luxurious cream puff, but it will plow through almost anything, as you saw. And you can almost get a cow in the trunk."

"So it's a working ranch limo for rich cowboys then," said Sam.

"Seems about right," Carl replied. They both chuckled at the idea.

Edna brought two tall glasses and set them before the two men at the table. She filled them with milk before leaving and then returned with their two plates. Sam saw a thick slice of cold meatloaf lying between the two slices of white bread. The rich smell of the meatloaf, combined with the sweet mayonnaise, caused his mouth to water. He remembered other meatloaf sandwiches in the past, provided by mothers, grandmothers, and aunts. He took a drink of milk and bit into the sandwich. Its savory flavor filled his mouth. He thought it was the best meatloaf sandwich he had ever tasted.

Edna, Carl, and Sam sat in the Gilinsky living room, sipping red wine. Sam thought it was a little sweet, but he had certainly drunk worse. In fact, he usually did.

The living room floors were beautiful old oak, like the hallway, finished to a satin shine while the center of the floor was covered with a lighter-colored Navajo area rug. Simple, dark-wood antique tables and chairs were mixed in with the newer couches and lounge chairs, one of which Sam now sat on. The Gilinskys, rather, shared a couch. A seventeen-inch Sony television sat on a shelf in a whole wall of shelves. Sam was comforted by the warmth of the crackling fire in the fireplace and the voice of Glenn Campbell that sang "Wichita Lineman" on the stereo.

Edna asked Sam about his home and family. He told her about leaving the Air Force Academy, but like Carl, she did not pry into the details. Her family had moved to Kansas in 1910 to open a dry goods store. She and Carl had met in high school and were married right after he returned from World War II. They were unable to have children.

"I guess I compensated for that by raising horses, goats, geese, dogs, and anything else we wouldn't eat," she said.

"Oh, I wouldn't say that," said Carl with a wink to Sam. "She's never needed an excuse to bring a critter into our house."

Edna was asking Carl about his day, but Sam was not following very well. He was fighting to keep his eyes open.

Carl looked at him. "Are you riding into the sunset again, Sam?"

Sam jerked himself awake. He wanted to be polite and attentive, but his whole body was weary.

"Afraid so. Sorry to be so rude."

"Well, you've been battling Mother Nature all day, and she can be a bitch in Kansas," said Carl.

"Oh Carl!" scolded Edna.

"Well, she can be," stated Carl, shrugging.

Looking at Sam, she said, "Hon, you come with me."

Sam struggled to get out of his chair. Edna led the way back to the entry hall. "You just leave that bag there for now, Sam. You can get it in the morning."

He was thankful not to have to drag the weight right now. He followed her up the stairs.

"The heat is not so good up here, son. I put on a few comforters to keep you warm."

Edna opened the first door to the right. Sam saw the corner room had windows on two sides. Snow was still falling outside, swarming around the outdoor light. A tall, antique wardrobe was against one windowless wall, and a double bed with two nightstands was against the other. One of the nightstand lamps was dimly lit. The room smelled like freshly washed linen.

"The bathroom's right across the hall, and there's washcloths and towels in there for you as well. Is there anything else I can get you?"

"Oh my gosh, no. That sandwich brought me back from the dead. You and Carl saved me tonight."

"You think I should keep him around then, huh?"

Sam shrugged. "Yeah, why not?"

Edna laughed. "Well," she said, patting his head, "you have sweet dreams."

He stripped down to his underwear. Edna was not kidding about the heating, so he quickly slid under the sheets. The sheet was almost stiff from the cold, and Sam felt his body heat being sucked out. He lay under almost a foot of multiple hand-stitched quilts, so he knew that his body would soon heat up the cocooned space. He shivered as the temperature slowly rose around him. Soon he was toasty.

Sam relaxed and sank deeper into the goose down mattress, thinking of long-lost ancient mammals roaming across the snowy plains.

17 ——————————— April 28, 1969

Sam woke to the smell of frying bacon and brewing coffee. He did not remember any sweet dreams, or any other dreams for that matter. But he remembered feelings of rescue, rest, and relief as he had sunk down into the soft mattress. In the nest that Edna had created, he had slept a much deeper sleep than he could remember having in a long time. He was now completely recharged and ready to take on anything once again.

He didn't get to sleep very much at the academy, or if he did, it was never long enough. He was always fighting to stay awake. He was not complaining, but he didn't sleep very much at Cheryl's either. Waking up in her arms was such comfort and bliss, but they still worked to maximize their conscious time together.

Being sleep-deprived by design, cadets tried to steal snatches of sleep whenever they could. Sam developed an ability to sleep while still listening to his surroundings. He would sink into a semi-awake state, but if he heard a sound like close footsteps, he could instantly snap to full consciousness. He could also sleep in a variety of positions. Since the door to his room was required to be open when he or Derek were there, whenever he needed to sneak a short nap, he would sit at his desk facing the open door and pretend he was reading a book. He would prop up his head with his hands on his forehead and his elbows locked, establishing a delicate balance while he slept.

One afternoon while napping, his mutant sense alarmed him, and he immediately awoke. Moments later, an upperclassman entered his room. He jumped up out of his chair, yelling, "Good afternoon, sir!" He stood stiffly at attention, but he could not feel anything in his right leg. It had gone to sleep. It turned out that he could not really control the leg either. Still at attention, he slowly tilted to the right until he fell over on the floor like a tree.

The upperclassman hesitated. Finally, he just broke out laughing and left.

Sam grabbed a quick shower in the Gilinskys' upstairs bathroom. Edna had laid out a fresh change of clothes from his bag. He dried off, shaved, and dressed rapidly. Feeling refreshed and clean, he went down the stairs and walked into the kitchen.

Edna was bustling around the kitchen, beating eggs in a bowl, and popping bread into a toaster. Carl was sitting at the dinette table, wearing glasses, sipping his coffee, and reading the paper.

"Good morning, Sam," chirped Edna. "Go sit down. Can I get you some coffee?"

Sam said, "Morning, Edna. Yeah, I could definitely use some, thank you."

Edna was wearing a white, long-sleeved blouse over black nylon pants. She was not going to be caught in her bathrobe again. Her light-brown hair was church-perfect, and her makeup was carefully applied.

He turned to the man at the table. "Morning, Carl."

"Morning, Sam," said Carl, putting down his coffee. "How'd you sleep?"

"Had a great night's sleep, thanks. Like I fell in a well."

Edna poured coffee into a large mug and placed it in front of Sam. "Cream or sugar?"

"Black is fine. Thank you."

"I hope you're hungry," she remarked.

"Absolutely." Sam sipped his coffee and sighed at its deep smell and taste.

Edna finished stirring the scrambled eggs and scooped them onto three plates. She took a platter of bacon warming in the oven and added several pieces to each. She put five pieces on Sam's plate and put the extra slice of toast on Sam's as well. Once she placed everything, she sat down. She looked back and forth at Sam and Carl, waiting.

"Well dig in, boys."

Sam spread a healthy portion of butter on his toast. He took a bite and followed up with a bite of eggs. "This is delicious, Edna. Seriously," Sam said, eyes closed in appreciation.

Edna beamed at him, and Carl raised his eyes above his newspaper and smiled. He laid down the paper and focused on his plate. Sam's sensation of well-being was deep and warm. He tried not to gulp down his breakfast like a ravenous wolf.

When they had finished eating and Edna poured coffee refills, Sam and Carl moved to the sunroom at the back of the house. Outside, Sam saw the sun was low, but bright, and he saw the snow sparkling with the ice that had formed in the night. He noticed a potbellied stove in the corner, popping and radiating heat.

"My grandfather and grandmother came here in 1870," Carl said, sitting in one of the sunroom chairs. "They came from Pennsylvania on the Shady Hill Trail and settled this land. Kansas had been a state for less than ten years at the time, can you believe that? And Oakley, Kansas, itself didn't even exist until the 1880s. There was still feuding from the Civil War as well as all that violence over slavery from before and during it too. We had family members on both sides. There were bad feelings for quite a while," he paused, contemplating a moment before continuing. "My grandparents ran cattle on about fifty thousand acres. You can imagine what this country was like in the late 1800s. They drove the herds to Wichita where the nearest railhead was. And they were tough, resilient people. Had to be. We now own only a small fraction of that original property, and we only have a few cattle and some horses. Edna breeds horses actually, but I have yet to see her ride one."

They smiled.

"How did the ranch get smaller?" asked Sam.

"A lot of reasons. As new settlers came in, they wanted to farm. Pieces of the ranch were sold to the farmers when times got tough. As Oakley became more of a town, my father preferred to work in town rather than being a rancher. I suspect a bigger reason was that more women were coming out here. He wanted to meet some of those women and find my mom. So, by the time I came along in 1919, this wasn't really much of a working ranch anymore. In any case, the ranch continued to shrink until today. Now we only own about forty acres.

"After the war, when I came back after I had left the navy, I worked in town at the auction yard. 'Cause I'm such a talented yeller, see, I eventually got the job of auctioneer there."

They chuckled.

"Now I travel around auctioning everything from livestock, to furniture, to useless lady stuff. It's been a good time, and it's interesting. The only times I don't like my work is when I conduct a foreclosure or bankruptcy sale. I know I'm not responsible for the poor people's pain, but I feel a little complicit in it."

They both gazed out the window at the sparkling snow.

Carl said, "If you don't mind me asking, what do you want to do with your life?"

Sam hesitated. "I don't know exactly. I just know for sure what I *don't* want to do, and that's to be in the military, and especially fighting in the Vietnam War." He reflected on what Carl would think of that after everything he had come to know about him. "I'm sorry. I greatly admire your service in World War II. My father was in the Pacific too." He stopped to think about how to describe his beliefs. "I just came to realize that the military demands from us"—he paused, thinking of the best wording to use before continuing—"unquestioned obedience, despite any concerns we might have for our own personal welfare. And that's the way it needs to be if you're going to win in battle. You can't tell soldiers to go over that hill and then let each soldier decide whether it's worth it or not. Or, you know, why not that hill over there instead?"

"That's right," said Carl.

Sam's hands twisted in his lap nervously at what he was going to say next. "But how can you go over that hill, which may get you killed, if you don't feel your home and country are really threatened? To me, that's the difference between serving in World War II and serving in Vietnam."

Carl sipped his coffee. "I understand your point, Sam. I hate war and violence of all sorts. But after Pearl Harbor, we all felt that Japan and Germany were on our doorsteps. It looked like they were going to take over the whole world. We were convinced that we were in a death struggle with the evil villains, you know? I truly believed I was obligated to join the struggle to save the world. I still feel that way too. I enlisted in the navy as soon as I could. I'd hardly been out of Kansas, so I thought maybe I could see the world too. I was a machinist mate on a destroyer in the Pacific."

They both took a sip of coffee.

"Don't kid yourself, Sam," he continued. "We weren't steely-eyed heroes with this overpowering will to win. Sure, we were all determined as we went off to enlist. But then reality hit, and we were just kids who were terrified, uncertain, and miserable. Sure, we all showed a different front on the outside, but that's what we were on the inside. We were aching to get back home." Carl paused. "Despite that, most of us fought pretty courageously, if I do say so myself."

"You should know that hearing you fought under those conditions of fear and suffering makes your actions even more noble to me," Sam said sincerely.

"Thanks, Sam, but I also think there's no such thing as a completely noble war. Even with the best intentions, the savagery around you makes you more of a savage yourself. That savagery was more in-your-face for those fighting on the ground than it was for me on a ship. My own fears rather came from being sunk and lost at sea." They stared out the window at the unblemished snowfield. Carl sighed. "I do see how you boys feel differently about Vietnam. And I see how you have a hard time staking your life on a dubious cause like that. Just because the enemies are communists? Never been a big believer in the domino theory of spreading communism myself. No, I don't think the threat from Vietnam is anywhere near the menace we all felt in World War II."

Sam nodded, glad Carl was at least being receptive to his own beliefs. "All I know at this point is that if I don't get back into college, I'll likely be going over that hill in Vietnam no matter what I believe. It's just important to me to avoid giving someone else the decision on whether I live or die for a cause I can't bring myself to feel much passion for." After that, they sat comfortably in silence and finished their coffees.

Later that morning, after having thanked Edna for everything, Sam and Carl rode south on US-83 toward Oakley. He saw some one-story houses and grain elevators but no larger-business buildings. Carl turned the big Lincoln left as US-83 merged with US-40 going east. The snow was melting rapidly due to the much warmer morning, and the streets were clear of the snow that had plagued it just recently. The ground was still covered, but the snow melted fast.

Carl parked the Lincoln near the entrance ramp to I-70. He looked with concern across at Sam. "Sam, I really think you'll be all right. You're a good, capable young man, and you'll find a way to work through this."

"Thanks for your faith in me, Carl."

As he watched the car pull away, Sam found himself finally starting to believe it.

18 —————————————— April 28, 1969

Sam stood under the I-70 overpass on the outskirts of Oakley, Kansas. It was cool and crisp. The sun had warmed the midmorning air to about sixty-five degrees. He thought the wind must be coming from the south now, bringing the warmth with it as the snow had almost melted and the runoff gurgled through the ditches and culverts as a result. He stretched and lifted his face to the sun. Birds sang in celebration of the warming day.

Wearing a long-sleeved work shirt over a T-shirt, he opened his bag to pack his peacoat, which was no longer needed. Edna had packed him a meatloaf sandwich and an apple in his bag and all his clothes were clean and neatly folded underneath. He smiled at her motherly nature.

He removed the wax paper from the sandwich and contentedly munched on it while he looked around. About a dozen hitchhikers sat or lay in groups on the slanted, concrete retaining wall, soaking up the sun's warmth. Sam recognized the young couple who had shared his Burlington, Colorado, highway ramp before his ill-fated ride with Leonard.

The woman was dressed in bell-bottom blue jeans and a long-sleeved peasant shirt. A jacket was tied around her waist. Her blonde hair was cropped short in a slightly more unkempt version of a Twiggy hairdo. She looked to be in her early twenties.

She was lying on her back on the wall incline, holding her fine, tanned face at an angle to fully catch the sun's rays. She was slim and delicate. Her breasts pressed against her shirt, reminding him once again of his love for the no-bra look. He relished the clean, fresh, natural beauty of the girls he was seeing everywhere he went. The man was dark haired and about Sam's size. His hair was parted in the middle, hanging straight down to around the bottom of his ears, and his dark mustache didn't end until below the corners of his mouth.

For the first time, Sam noticed that there was a small dog with them. He saw that it was not on a leash but looked content enough to stay right by their sides. He thought the dog was a cocker spaniel. Its dark ginger coat was short on its back and face and somewhat longer and curlier on its underside, ears, and legs. The dog's bobbed tail twitched excitedly as the woman offered it a bit of food. He wondered where the dog was when he saw the couple in Burlington.

Sam strolled over to them. "I see you haven't got any further than I did."

The man answered, "No, we haven't. We stood on that entrance ramp forever as the weather got shittier. We were lucky to find a sleezy motel room. We got a ride here this morning."

"Hey, I think I know just the one. I'm Sam," he said, holding out his hand.

The man shook Sam's hand. "I'm Jon, and this is Michele," he said, pointing to her.

"Glad to meet you," said Sam, bending down and shaking her outstretched hand. He reached over to pet the dog, who licked his hand. "And who's this?"

"This is Heidi," said Michele in a light, cheerful voice.

"I didn't see her in Burlington. Where was she?"

"She's a smart dog," said Michele. "When it's cold and windy outside, she gets inside one of our bags to ride it out."

Sam said, "Now that's impressive. How does that work out? You hitchhiking with her?"

"She knows just what to do," she said. "She just poses cutely in front of us while we stick our thumbs out, and she looks beseechingly at the drivers. She's our ride bait." In her baby dog voice, holding Heidi's head in both hands, she added, "Who can pass up such a beautiful dog?"

Jon shrugged. "She really does increase our chances of a ride. We probably would've found a ride yesterday if she hadn't been in the bag."

Heidi barked. Sam thought she understood she was the center of the conversation. Michele stroked her behind her ears, and Heidi's eyes looked at Michele adoringly. It was only when Michele stopped petting her that Heidi waddled over and found a soft spot to lay down.

Sam asked, "So where'd you come from, and where're you going?"

"We're originally from Madison, Wisconsin," Jon said, gesturing behind him with his thumb. "We were going to San Francisco in our Volkswagen Beetle with all our stuff on a roof rack. We really wanted to be a part of that whole scene. Coming across America in our old bug felt like doing it with a covered wagon. What an adventure, man!" he said and then looked outwards toward the road, as if reliving it all over again.

"I'll never forget driving all that way across the plains and seeing the first of the Rockies to the west," Michele chimed in. "We were so thrilled. And it got better and better as we got closer. I'd seen pictures, but they were nothing like the real thing."

"And climbing those mountains was amazing," Jon added. "The bug never got out of second gear for the whole climb. We drove through the Wasatch Range into Utah, past the Great Salt Lake and the Great Basin."

"I don't know how the people in the real covered wagons made it," said Michele, shaking her head and leaning over to pet Heidi again who had dozed off.

"Then came the Cascade Range, which was even more mind-blowing than the Rockies," said Jon.

"First it blew our minds, and then it blew our transmission," Michele said. She laughed and shrugged.

"Good thing we were on the western slope when the transmission died," said Jon, chuckling and looking over at her. "We put the Volkswagen in neutral and just coasted for miles and miles. It would've been fun if we weren't so bummed about the car. We ended up in Truckee, California.

Rolled right into the gas station. The guy at the station told us he was just closing up and that he couldn't look at our car until the next morning."

Michele piped in, "He also told us that he happened to have a Volkswagen minibus behind the gas station that he was working on, and we were welcome to hole up there for the night." She paused, smiling and reminiscing. "That was the most luxurious place to sleep that we'd encountered on our whole trip. It had beautiful wood paneling and a super comfy bed in the back. The night was beautiful . . . and so romantic, wasn't it?"

"It was. But before we went to bed," Jon continued, "we walked toward town to find a pay phone to call our friends in San Francisco, right? We asked if they could come get us if the bug was declared dead. They told us they couldn't leave until morning, and it would take them about four hours to get to Truckee. We said that would work, and we would call them back when we got the verdict on the VW."

"Armed with that plan," said Michele, "we wandered the mostly closed town center until we found a liquor store and bought a six-pack of Colt 45 'Tallboy' malt liquors. We both thought it was the appropriate response to the situation we were in, you know?"

"That's fair," grinned Sam. "Can't say I wouldn't do the same."

"Thank you! So anyways, we walked back to the gas station and took up residence in our car so we could at least listen to the radio. After a few malt liquors, we wanted to see if the car might've cured itself, so Jon started it up. It still ran fine. But if he let out the clutch in any forward gear, the car just sat there. It would move normally in reverse though. Jon was pretty sure the transmission was dead. So we spent a few hours cruising backward around the gas station, listening to faint radio stations and drinking our Tallboys."

Jon laughed. "Turned out to be a pretty good warm-up to 'Love in the Hotel Minibus.'"

Michele punched him in the arm, rolling her eyes.

Sam asked, "And where's Heidi during all of this?"

"Oh, Heidi always just hangs out with Michele, no matter what's going on," said Jon. "I swear the two of them could walk down the streets of New York City and Heidi would never leave her side, leash or no leash."

"She's my baby," cooed Michele. She patted her thigh and Heidi, now awake at the mention of her name, came running. Michele hugged her.

Jon said, "The next morning the mechanic looked over the Beetle and pronounced that it did indeed need a new transmission, which would cost more than the car was worth. He said he could always use another source of Volkswagen parts, though. He gave us fifty bucks, and we drove it backward to get it behind the station. We called our friends, moved our luggage rack and stuff to their car and headed west. Just left the keys in the Beetle."

"I assume you made it to San Francisco without any other issue, yeah?" Sam asked. "So how come you're not there now? Not what you thought it would be?"

Michele paused before answering. "We wanted to, and we did stay for a while. It was wild out there. You felt like you were at the center of the universe. There was such joy and freedom. You passed people in the street who greeted you and acknowledged their connection to you. Musicians played outside in the sun." But Michele's expression suddenly darkened a little. "But it was so crowded. Everyone and their dogs were there. We were just another couple and another dog, you know? Actually, crowded doesn't cut it. People were actually living on the streets. And Jon and I are used to sleeping outside, don't get me wrong, but the trash and smell were a bit much sometimes."

"Right," said Jon. "There were so many people, you could forget all about getting a job and a place to live, especially without a car. Once our welcome ran out with our friends, our only choices were to take to the streets ourselves or head back to Madison and lick our wounds. We tried to make do on the streets, thinking surely it was temporary. Michele was a waitress. I bartended. I tried to get some construction jobs, but there wasn't much. Not enough for rent and a car, anyway. Bottom line, I'd say San Francisco is a place where we'd love to live, but I'll be damned if I know how we'd pay for it."

Michele smiled and spread her arms over their surroundings. "So, lick our wounds it is, and here we are, in beautiful Oakley, Kansas."

Sam thought their adventurous and optimistic spirit was contagious. He could almost feel it himself. He admired their courage to strike out for a shot at the futures they sought. Sam couldn't help but think of the similarities between their journey and the westward odysseys of the pioneers. Except one was littered with more dead transmissions and VWs rather than dead wagons, livestock, and pioneers.

19 ——————————— April 28, 1969

After saying goodbye and good luck to Jon and Michele, Sam stood on the I-70 entrance ramp, his bag at his side. It was sunny, just warm enough to shed his work shirt but with a light breeze to cool it down.

As if Michele had conjured it out of the air, Sam saw an old Volkswagen minibus laboring up the ramp's slight incline toward him. It pulled over and stopped a few feet in front of him. The minibus was painted turquoise on the bottom and white on the top, which continued down the front of the vehicle to a point like a nose. When combined with its beady headlights and smiling, white front bumper, the front resembled a cute cartoon face like that of an animal.

Sam walked to the passenger side. Half of the front side window was slid forward, sharp acrid smoke drifting out of the opening. Sam heard the 5th Dimension sing "Aquarius" on the radio.

The window section slid in front of the other section the rest of the way like a sliding shower door. A long-haired man stuck his head out of it and smiled widely. "Greetings, noble traveler!" he shouted. "Can we provide you with transportation?"

"Sure!" Sam shouted back.

Sam heard a metallic *clunk,* and the right half of the double doors on the passenger side swung out. Sam threw his bag onto the floor between the front and back seats and then lifted himself inside.

"What's your name, wanderer?" asked the man in the shotgun position.

"Sam Roberts. What about you guys?"

"My friends call me Moon Daddy," the passenger said, "but if that doesn't roll off your tongue, you can call me Moon. Our esteemed pilot here is Ziggy."

"Great to meet you both."

"Just make yourself at home," said Ziggy.

Moon looked to be a little taller than Sam and almost as stringy. His long reddish-blond hair was parted in the middle and held tightly against his skull by a headband. From there, his hair erupted out in a frizz from his head onto his shoulders. He sported a stubby red beard and mustache on his ruddy cheeks. He could have passed for a Viking warrior had he not been wearing a faded-blue, peace-sign-emblazoned T-shirt.

Ziggy was more compact and muscular with a darker complexion. His black hair was in a shaggy afro which framed his face in tight curls, and his bushy mustache extended down to his jaw line. Sam noticed a tattoo of an eagle carrying an American flag on his right bicep.

Sam looked around the interior. It was simple with its German "you don't really need that" practicality. What the Germans did provide was ingenious and meticulously engineered. Sam saw eight back windows. All but the two back ones were hinged on the back side and could be popped out a certain way. While moving, each window would scoop the air breezily into the cabin.

Sam had always liked the wind in his face in a car ride, but he couldn't help but wonder how the open windows, along with the windshield window—which looked like it could be independently propped open from the bottom—stayed on when cruising down the interstate.

The front bucket seats and the two rear bench seats were two-toned gray vinyl, as was the door's interior trim. With the engine in the rear of the bus, the driver and front passenger sat with their knees close to the actual front of the minibus. The metal dashboard contained only a radio, speedometer, and gas gauge. Sam felt that riding in the minibus was a combination of Lindberg flying across the Atlantic and an RAF pilot flying his plane with his wing on fire.

Ziggy started up the minibus. The engine sounded like a lawn mower behind Sam, and it seemed he could hear each explosion in the cylinders. Ziggy revved the engine a few times to make sure it would keep running, then put the long floor-mounted stick shift into first. He pulled away and slowly accelerated, shifting into higher gears when the engine seemed about to explode.

Minutes passed before they reached fifty mph. The open windows in the minibus rattled as they reached full speed, but they remained securely hinged to the minivan and continued to scoop the air through the cabin.

"You have to let Hans take his time," Ziggy said, patting the steering wheel. "He's in it for the long haul."

Moon said, "Since we're going east, we're going downhill with the wind. So maybe we'll get to fifty-five."

"Or maybe we can draft behind a semi and go eighty," suggested Ziggy.

They rode along and exchanged small talk for a bit. Sam found out that Moon and Ziggy had been living on a communal farm in Oregon. It had not worked out for whatever reason, and they were now traveling from Oregon to another commune in Virginia called Twin Oaks, but they were stopping near Kansas City to see some friends first. Before living in the Oregon commune, Ziggy was in the army in Vietnam and Moon had lived in Portland, so they hadn't become friends until they had worked together in a Portland restaurant. Sam finally told them he had just quit the Air Force Academy.

"Right on!" cheered Moon. "Let's celebrate your good sense!"

Moon opened the glove compartment and reached back into it. Sam heard a series of clicks and pops. Moon pulled out a joint.

Ziggy laughed. "Moon built a secret compartment in there. Works great too. You can't see shit even when you're up close."

"Have you needed it?" asked Sam.

Moon snorted. "Uh yeah! I mean, look at us. I venture to say we get more than our fair share of police attention."

"It's not always friendly attention, either," said Ziggy, glancing at him seriously. "Earlier this trip, in the middle of 'No Name,' Utah, we didn't come to a full stop at the bottom of an exit ramp. A less-than-cheerful town constable pulled us over, wrote us a ticket, and demanded forty dollars in cash to avoid a courtroom appearance. Even told us that we'd need to attend a small class in 'stop-sign management.' He made us sit and wait in front of the stop sign for an hour, while he parked behind us and ate his lunch. For dessert, he searched the minibus while we waited on the side of the road."

"He ran his hands all through the glove compartment and looked right at the secret compartment," said Moon, a slight amount of pride in his voice. "He didn't see a thing. Unless they bring dogs, I'm pretty sure we're cool." He lit the joint and pulled a huge volume of smoke deep into his lungs. "You up for this?" Moon croaked while holding his breath. He held the joint back out to Sam.

Sam had sought out the good times and found drinking to be an easy way to help get them. At the age of fifteen, he and his friends met at night in a sand trap at Green Briar golf course. They drank heisted warm beer and smoked cigarettes to compensate for not being able to drive and losing their girlfriends to guys who could. At least, that was their excuse to each other for sitting in the dark, sipping beers and swatting mosquitos. Most of them took up smoking on the theory that it kept the bugs away. The rest of them also took up smoking to be cool, especially when they secretly considered themselves anything but.

Sam continued drinking throughout high school. It was the social lubricant that made music sound better and girls easier to talk to. Although he only drank on some weekends and considered himself a moderate drinker, on some Saturday nights, he might have gotten a little carried away.

He had been stopped numerous times by the Kirkwood police. They knew him personally and knew that while Sam was a little wild, he was not destructive and would not willingly hurt anyone. Being an air force brat, he was naturally polite with authorities and quick with the "yes, sirs." The policemen would just pat him on the head and tell him, "Go straight home, son, and be careful."

But at the Air Force Academy, drinking opportunities were rare. And while they hardly ever happened, when they did, the fourth classmen were never left alone to drink anyway. Even upperclassmen could not openly drink alcohol on academy grounds.

When cadets were temporarily released to the outside world, they naturally were motivated to have the best time possible in the shortest amount of time. In an attempt to recreate the good times they remembered, they emerged from the academy like wild dogs chasing down an elk.

But Sam had not used marijuana yet. He did not think it was immoral, despite having been forced, as an adolescent, to watch the movie *Reefer Madness* at the YMCA. And besides, first time for everything.

"Sure, man," Sam answered and took the joint from Moon.

"There you go, man!" said Moon. "I always figured there are little kids who like to spin around until they fall over and little kids who don't. I think the spinners grow up to love marijuana. I'm definitely a spinner. You look like a spinner to me."

Sam took a long, deep hit on the joint as he saw Moon do. He felt fire in his throat and immediately started coughing violently.

"Easy, pilgrim," Ziggy chuckled. "Looks like we got a virgin here, Moon."

Once the fire in his throat subsided, Sam took another tentative hit on the joint and handed it to Ziggy. After several rounds, Moon turned back to Sam and asked, "Feeling anything yet, pilgrim?"

He shook his head. Sam thought he did not feel much aside from a light, pleasant pressure between his eyes. He couldn't help but admire the finely crafted window hardware and marveled how well the music sounded on the radio. He couldn't stop smiling as he looked out the front window. They were going way too fast, in his opinion, although he couldn't find reason enough to care. He laughed uproariously at one of Moon's jokes, even though right after he said it, he couldn't remember why he found it so funny in the first place.

"What about now?" Moon asked again, grinning back at him.

"Not much yet," Sam answered.

.

Ziggy and Moon looked at each other and laughed.

The radio began playing the Moody Blues' "Ride My Seesaw." Even coming from the Volkswagen's tinny radio speaker, Sam had not ever heard music that sounded better.

His father was always a sucker for new technology and gleefully always bought the latest gadgets. He was a stereo pioneer, owning one of the first systems in 1960. It had a giant Sansui amplifier made from thick sheet metal and filled with glowing tubes. It weighed about seventy-five pounds.

But his parents only used it to listen to bland orchestral music. As a kid, Sam endured long car rides when, during these occasions, he was a captive, greatly bored audience member in the back seat. When they could, Sam and his sisters sought refuge with soul music and popular rock 'n' roll.

But music was not that inspiring to Sam in the late fifties and early sixties. He had other things on his mind. The AM radio stations played a very limited library of hits that were all less than two minutes long, chopped the songs off for a commercial before they were done, and invaded the song beginnings with frenetic DJ chatter. Although soul music and California surf music were more absorbing, most of what the radio played was incessant pop songs, the mainstream music—bland and predictable.

That all changed in the mid-1960s with the British Invasion. The Beatles, Rolling Stones, and other English groups hit the airways. American bands soon followed their leads. It was a gale of fresh air for Sam and his friends. While AM radio was still filled with manic DJs and cut-off short songs and FM radios (which not many owned, especially in their cars) played mostly classical music, St. Louis finally became home to one of the first FM stations, KSHE, to play whole rock albums from artists who were not necessarily Top 40.

There were limited commercials and hardly any talk. The longer the song, the better. When a DJ had to talk, he was calm and cool. Sam was lucky to drive a car with an FM radio, which served him well on dates, parking and sipping on gin fizzes while relishing the tunes. The music was finally exotic, captivating, and lively.

During Sam's high school years, music became a common language for most teenagers. There were so many great groups to choose from. The pace of album releases accelerated, with most groups producing several albums per year. Even the quality of the music was astounding. Sam and his friends bought new albums from their favorite artists without even listening to them first, and friends gathered to share their favorite new music on their parents' stereos.

Sam still sensed that the rock music renaissance was continuing. There was a dizzying number of artists who were inspired to produce original masterpieces. He and Cheryl spent many hours cuddling up to their favorite music, feeling an electric connection through their skin that caused the beat and melody to flow easily between them.

They sung as the preacher urged the congregation to come forward, be saved, and join the church. Reverend Johnson would pause the hymn at the end of each verse and extoll the congregation to come forward, save themselves, and seek forgiveness. "The Old Rugged Cross" had four long verses, which was an ominous sign to the two siblings. Reverend Johnson also stopped the singing when someone came up, causing Kay to groan in disgust.

"Don't do it!" she whispered as a lady across the aisle appeared to be steeling herself to approach the altar.

The last verse came to an end. Reverend Johnson looked around the altar and was clearly not satisfied with the size of his flock. "Any one of us could pass on at any time. None of us is guaranteed another moment of earthly existence. We must all be saved and prepared to meet our God, maybe just on the other side of that door," he shouted, pointing to the church door itself.

He paused and remained silent until some were about to bolt forward just to ease the tension.

"I want to give another chance to you who are considering coming forward. We will start again at verse one."

"God no," whispered Kay. "Not a repeat."

The organ started, and the congregation began hesitantly. Most of them probably didn't appreciate the repeat either.

"I can't take it!" growled Kay as she shoved Sam out of the pew and into the aisle. She must have hoped sacrificing her brother would free all of them.

He was not expecting her shove and was already off-balance. He stumbled down the aisle into the space between the front and back sections of pews, crashing loudly enough to be clearly heard above the mumbled singing. The hymn stopped, and everyone turned. Sam looked around, started back to his seat, hesitated, and eventually headed for the altar.

He had faked his conversion.

Ziggy laughed. "Surely you're going to hell for that one." After a pause, Ziggy asked, "You believe in reincarnation?" Sam thought again about his time in Taiwan and realized that it was all the way back then that he had come to know there were other paths to the same truths, even if he hadn't realized it at the time.

"I don't know," Sam said. "Christians may not believe it, but it makes a certain amount of sense to me. It's hard to imagine all the souls since the beginning of time just hanging out in heaven or hell. Like what are they doing? Just laying around on the clouds in heaven, playing harps? Waiting for an angel assignment? I'm not sure exactly. Reincarnation seems a lot like soul recycling—the circle of life and all that. In any case, I find it hard to believe God will cast us into hell over believing, or not believing, the minor details."

"I'm a little embarrassed to tell you guys this, but I know one thing, man," Moon said. "If I'm reincarnated, I want to come back as something with a bigger dick."

Sam and Ziggy looked at each other, then snorted and laughed. They stopped to catch their breath, then were laughing again.

"You dumb shit!" hooted Ziggy. "Think about it. You could come back as a whale with a dick as long as this minibus. But all the other whales would still laugh at you in the whale locker room because theirs are as long as school buses."

"Yeah, Moon," added Sam as he dried his eyes. "You better be more specific with your wishes. God loves irony."

He had once asked a Sunday School teacher if Mahatma Gandhi was in hell because he was not Christian. The teacher thought he was, and Sam skipped out on Sunday School for a year. He thought that, in the history of Christianity, tolerance was not exactly a cornerstone. The Crusades, the Inquisition, they all were testaments to that. Many Christians were even intolerant of other Christians. Sam knew that some other religions also shared this trait, so perhaps his problem was with all organized religion, not just Christianity. It was something to think about for him as he listened to the wind whipping through the minibus and as the land rolled by. Perhaps he hadn't figured out all of his beliefs just yet. But that was OK. There was still time. But he knew one thing: he believed that a church's primary purpose should be to improve the world in whatever ways they can . . . and to teach others to do the same.

21 ———————————— April 28, 1969

The turquois minibus chugged along I-70. Sam gazed out the panoramic windows, some of which were cracked open. Ever so gradually, the flat countryside was transitioning to low hills. He noticed the trees were becoming taller and more numerous. The budding of the trees was further along than on the higher plains to the west, and grass in the pastures reflected an iridescent green glow of new growth. Sam smelled dirt arising from freshly turned fields.

The radio news was describing how the Vietcong were reported to be concentrating in certain areas of the northern parts of South Vietnam and across the border in North Vietnam. Army Intelligence believed the Vietcong were preparing for an offensive later in the spring but theorized that they thought the South Vietnamese Army had improved their capabilities to be able to defend themselves, allowing US troops to draw down.

"You believe that shit?" yelled Ziggy. "That's about the hundredth time we've heard that drivel. The South Vietnamese Army is never going to be able to go toe-to-toe with the Vietcong. I'm not saying there are not some good South Vietnamese soldiers, just not enough of them to go it alone. The Vietcong are brutal, and I certainly wouldn't root for a lot of the shit they pull, but Ho Chi Minh has been fighting for Vietnamese independence since 1941. He fought on our side in World War II, for God's sake. In any case, the Vietnamese need to come up with their own damn solutions. It's not our job to figure it out. It's not our fucking fight!" He hit the steering wheel. "But we keep sending more boys over there anyway!"

"And the killing goes on," said Moon morosely.

They watched the country slide by. Sam felt he was finally taking actions to avoid killing or being killed. He was unsure if his actions would ultimately succeed, but he was doing something. That was comforting in its own small way.

"Vietnam is such a fucking shithole," continued Ziggy. "I was drafted into the infantry, assigned to go out on useless patrols, trying to flush Vietcong from the jungle, right? But they were damn good at hiding, except when they wanted to take pot shots at us. Winning and holding territory didn't even seem to be our objectives. It was all about body counts. Your mission was considered a victory by the brass if you killed enough Vietcong, or whatever looked like them enough." He took a great heave of air before continuing.

"When we weren't on patrol, we sat around in our tents with little more to do than wait for the next one. The weather was either sticky and hot or rainy and cold. You couldn't get dry. When you were brave enough to look, you could watch your own skin peel away from the jungle rot. It was either boredom or terror, man. Anybody could start shooting at you at almost any time from behind a million bushes and trees. And almost every single damn day I saw things I will never be able to forget. Death was everywhere, and it was sudden. I saw men exploding and what bullets can do to flesh. Bodies from both sides just lay there, rotting right in the sun. Oh God, the smell!" He shivered.

Sam was almost too horrified to say anything. What would he even say? It seemed like Moon was having similar thoughts. Not daring to break the spell that seemed to envelope them, Sam let Ziggy continue.

"Most of the time, we outnumbered them. But sometimes we were surprised and had to fight larger numbers. Once we were about to be overrun when our planes dropped napalm on them. We were saved, and all that was left of them was human charcoal. That's a sight burned into my brain that I won't ever be able to get out."

He paused as he tried to rein in his emotions. "One time I was pinned down during a firefight in an open sewage ditch. Sure the smell was terrible, but it was preferable to being shot. I was about to duck my head in the shit water as the bullets were zinging over my head when a long-ass black snake dropped out of a tree right in front of me. God, I hate snakes, and Vietnam has some badass, fucking deadly snakes! It swam right at me, and I managed to push it away with my rifle. It started to swim away, but then turned back. I almost ran out of the water—damn the bullets over my head."

"What the hell did you do?" asked Sam.

"I shot the hell out of the snake with my M16 on full auto," Ziggy said, "then dove back under the shit water."

"Holy crap! How could you do that every day?" asked Sam in astonishment.

"It was not like that every day, thank God. Nothing really happened on a lot of the patrols, but they were still tense. Much of our time was doing nothing. This was when we rested up and tried to forget the horror of everything. We sometimes went to Saigon for leave, but those days are a haze. We drank and used drugs as much as we could to dull the stress and pain. We eventually found the Vietnamese prostitutes who pretended they loved us.

"It didn't take too long for me to stop believing the crap about 'mom and apple pie.' I wasn't buying the notion that we were defending the free world from communism. These guys weren't about to attack our ranches back home like the Apaches. What kept me going was the loyalty and love of my brothers. We patrolled together, ate together, slept together . . . shit together. Not one of us would have hesitated to risk our life to save a brother, even if we didn't particularly like him. Our platoon was like a living organism with all the body parts working together, without a damn pause." Ziggy hesitated. "I was aching to get home, but I miss those brothers. And I really missed them when I got home. It's not like we got any ticker-tape parades. It was either indifference or straight hostility."

"I don't understand how people can blame you soldiers for following the orders of our government," said Sam. "It's not like you created the war, man. You were just unlucky enough to be drafted to serve in it. You did your best and fought with honor. You deserve our thanks and respect, Ziggy."

Ziggy thought a little more about this.

"Thanks, Sam. The only positive thought I have from that fucked-up mess is that we all saved lives and had our own lives saved too. The thought comforts me a little."

"The brotherhood of man, man!" concluded Moon dreamily. He lit another joint. After exhaling the smoke, Moon said, "I would have been in the same boat as Ziggy if not for this toe thing I have. It doesn't bother me at all, but it was good for a 4F deferment." Moon reached for his foot. "Here. Let me show you."

"That's OK, Moon," said Ziggy, shoving his hand down. "You can spare us that."

Although Sam's bonds with his fellow cadets were not as visceral as Ziggy's were, he had to admit he missed them. One of the differences though with Sam's relationship with his cadets was that grunts had few opportunities to just hang out. Other than with their roommates, fourth classmen had little time to have anything relating to deep conversations with each other. Their friendships were forged from shared adversity and from facing that adversity together.

Some of the teamwork they did was deliberately and officially imprinted by the air force through designed team exercises, such as the team obstacle course. On this course, he and his mates went through a series of situations such as being confronted with a pretend destroyed bridge across a pretend radioactive river, equipped with nothing but a rope and a towel. The team then had to devise a way to get everyone across to the other side. Sam actually loved those exercises. It felt like recess.

Some of the other teamwork was fostered through sports. One memorable game was pushball. Pushball involved a hollow ten-foot-diameter ball and two teams of fifteen. The ball was placed in the middle of the field while the two teams, wearing nothing but shorts and T-shirts, started ten yards away from it. On the whistle, both teams charged full speed at the ball, and the melee erupted.

The point of the game was to push the giant ball past the opponent's goal line. There were no timeouts or period breaks, and there were no substitutions for the fallen. Those were the only rules in pushball.

There were three positions: (1) The largest guys were pushers. They pushed the ball against the other team's pushers to move the ball toward the opponent's goal line. (2) Cutters ran to the other team's side of the ball to cut down their pushers. (3) And then there were blockers, who knocked the shit out of cutters to keep them off their pushers. Sam was a blocker. Once one side gained the momentum, the ball accelerated down the field, knocking over the other side's players like bowling pins. The game was like a medieval battle but without the armor. Luckily his only injury was a bite mark on his calf, which he still didn't really have any idea how that had happened. But in terms of injuries, others were not so lucky to have missed so many.

The third leg of team building was stunts. Some were encouraged to build initiative and team spirit; others, not so much. Several were even frowned upon. Every cadet was a mixture of both boy and man, and stunts tended to bring out the dominance of the boy.

Sam recalled when he and about a thousand fourth classmen showed up in the middle of the night to push a display jet near the chapel all the way to the hallowed upper-class air gardens at the opposite side of the terrazzo, where grunts were considered trespassers. The jet was an actual test plane from the late 1940s, although its engine and much of the interior equipment had been removed. Yet it remained both historic and irreplaceable.

The mass of cadets manually pushed the jet all the way across the terrazzo, a distance made much larger considering the task. Construction scaffolding was "borrowed" and used to support the jet for the final move across a narrow bridge to the Air Garden's sacred fountain. The cadets lifted the plane onto the rolling scaffolding, pushed it across, then lifted the plane off it at its new home. They returned the scaffolding to its construction site and cleaned up, as if it had never happened. The academy awoke to the plane looking pristine in its new spot, no one having a clue as to how it showed up there. In the end, the authorities seemed to appreciate the initiative and must have thought it looked fine in its new home, so it stayed.

Another stunt involved arrows tied to a fishing line being fired over the chapel, raising a large BEAT ARMY banner. At least that one was popular and in the right spirit. Not every stunt had the same effect. When the Naval Academy's goat mascot was kidnapped when they came to play football, the academy seemed to believe this stunt to have been the one that had taken things too far. Sam had played no part, but it didn't matter. The entire student body was confined to their rooms over it.

And perhaps some of the team mischief was considered minor larceny. Sam's roommate, Derek, was the mastermind of a shadow organization of fourth classmen. He developed certain methods to gain information and spread instructions among the grunts, who were normally forbidden to talk to one another.

One of the organization's biggest operations was the soda/candy black market. This part found success because of the rarity of such items. Fourth classmen could not get these items anywhere, except maybe through some care packages from home. With a customer base of young men who had not touched such fare in months, a single soda or candy bar could fetch $5.

This operation involved a team of six spaced throughout the halls who would pretend to go to the shower or bathroom but were acting as lookouts. Shouting their greetings to upperclassmen was an alert to the insertion team. Consisting of Derek and Sam, the insertion team would then attack the forbidden vending machines. While pretending to be throwing away their trash in the trash chute, Sam would maniacally feed quarters into the machine, during which Derek pulled handles and filled the wastebaskets with the sodas and candy bars. They were most tense during the return mission to their room with still-full trash cans, which covered their contraband buried underneath. It was another challenge altogether to hide their inventory, given room inspections. But they managed.

Derek's web of informants, known only to him, was astounding. He seemed to have something on upperclassmen, enlisted air force personnel, and even officers. One day, Derek received word from an informant that their squadron's upperclassmen were planning a five-mile punishment run for the next morning at six, requiring full fatigues and gear.

The next morning, about fifty fourth classmen met in the dark at five thirty in full fatigues and ran around the nearest hill. The cadets loitered, smoking cigarettes and milling around until about a quarter after six when they got in marching formation and ran back around the hill to the front of their dorm. A few upperclassmen met them. It was now too late to run and still make breakfast.

"Where the hell have you been?" one upperclassman yelled.

Derek yelled back while at stiff attention, "Took ourselves on an exercise run, sir!"

Sam couldn't help but be impressed.

22 ———————————— April 28, 1969

Sam snapped awake on the middle bench seat of the minibus. The metallic chugging of the engine was combined with the sound of the whistling wind. He sat up and gazed around. The scenery had changed. His view to the right was dense tree fields for a bit. The trees blocked all further views, but they soon expanded when the minibus crossed into open land. Factories and chemical plants littered several of the open fields. Occasionally, he saw glimpses of a sluggish brown river to the south. The land rose on the north side of the road, punctuated with scattered, low cliff faces, and Sam smelled the flowers of spring mixed with the unidentifiable industrial odors. On the radio, The Zombies sang "Time of the Season."

Sam yawned and stretched his arms.

"Welcome back, stone cadet!" said Moon. "You were knocked out. Must have been the combination of our great Oregon weed and the mind-numbing scenery of Kansas."

"Yeah," added Ziggy, "Mind-numbing doesn't quite cover it. They raised the speed limit back there to seventy-five just because there was nothing we could possibly run into. Hans politely declined." He patted the dashboard lovingly. "We're just now rolling into Kansas City and will cross over into Missouri in a few minutes," he then instructed, imitating an airline pilot on the intercom.

A red pickup truck raced up on them in the left lane and then stayed alongside the minibus. Two men were in the seats. The passenger rolled down the window.

"Get your hippie asses out of Kansas!" the man yelled.

The truck sped up and then swerved abruptly back into the minibus's lane. Ziggy had to stomp on the brakes and swerve right to avoid being hit.

"Ya slobbering redneck cretins!" yelled Ziggy with his fist out the window. "Go fuck yourselves!"

"Yeah, assholes," Moon yelled. "Whatever happened to 'live and let live'?"

Unfortunately, the truck was well out of hearing.

"What do you think they have against minibuses?" asked Moon, frowning.

"C'mon, Moon," said Ziggy. "You know being a hippie is kinda like volunteering to be black. I haven't heard of a hippie getting lynched yet, but we get some of the same hateful looks and bullshit behavior."

"It's funny," said Moon. "If we hippies just cut our hair and changed our clothes, all that hostility and prejudice just goes away. Poof, like magic. Black men can't do that."

"In both cases," said Ziggy, "people are judging you and hating you based only on how you look. How stupid is that."

"God help you if you're a black hippie," concluded Moon, and Ziggy nodded.

Interstate 70 curved to the north to follow the Kansas River. The concentration of factories increased. As they turned east again and crossed the Kansas River, the view opened up to a wide, industrial expanse with the downtown skyline beyond the factories and warehouses emerging straight ahead. The sound of clanging metal and loud machinery came from inside.

"This looks like a town where they get shit done," Moon said.

"Now we're in Missouri," Ziggy said as they went over the bridge.

He watched as a road sign, which read GARMENT DISTRICT, flew past. Sam saw numerous old brick factories, many looking abandoned and with modest homes of working families sprinkled throughout. The neighborhood had some beautiful buildings itself as well, but there were also crumbling signs of decay.

Sam felt the familiarity of the environment in which he was raised. He could see bushes in the forests sprouting flowers in vibrant yellows and pinks and forests filled with thick broadleaf trees clumped throughout. As he inhaled an intoxicating, flowery, green fragrance, he couldn't help but compare it to the evergreen world of Colorado. But here, right now, it was only about eighty degrees. Sam had fallen asleep on a brisk, semi-barren high plain and had awoken in "Lush Land."

"God, do I love Missouri in the spring!" He couldn't help but laugh appreciatively, still almost shocked he was getting to do this.

Looking ahead, they saw the red pickup on the side of the road. The two men were changing the left rear tire. Moon stuck his head out the window and waited until the minivan was even with the truck. "Get cocky, get burnt, assholes!" he yelled. "Karma can be a bitch, man!"

Ziggy added a friendly series of toots from the minivan's horn.

Ziggy filled the minibus with gas at the Independence, Missouri, exit. They split the $4.20 three ways.

"Hey, Ziggy, let's hit up that chicken place across the road," yelled Moon, pointing at the restaurant across from them.

Sam looked at the restaurant called Kwik Chik and then looked incredulously at Moon, picturing ski masks and pistols. "No way!" he said. "Look, guys. It's been fun, but definitely not doing that."

Moon looked confused for a moment at the dawning horror on Sam's face and then laughed. "No, man, you don't understand. I don't mean, like, rob it. I mean check out their garbage."

"What the hell," said Sam. Certainly better than robbing it, but maybe not by much.

Ziggy turned to Sam and said, "You need to listen to Moon. He happens to be a trash-can connoisseur of great renown." Moon nodded his solemn appreciation.

And that's how Sam found himself in the bus, all three of them sitting low in their seats. Ziggy had parked up the street from the back of the Kwik Chik, far enough away to avoid notice.

A few minutes after seven in the evening, three teenagers came out of the back door carrying trash bags. They walked to the dumpster, threw the bags inside, and went back in. A few minutes later, the lights went off on the Kwik Chik sign, followed by the inside lights. Four figures soon came out the back door into the dark. One locked the door and then they all got into their cars and drove away. For a few minutes more, Sam, Ziggy and Moon sat in the bus, watching for any sign of movement. It was silent except for some chirping insects and distant traffic.

Moon bolted from the bus, crouching low and zigzagging across the street. He stopped a few times and lifted his head, swiveling it around to sense his surroundings like an animal would. When he reached the back of the Kwik Chik, he waved toward the bus and signaled Sam and Ziggy to follow. They ran, also crouched, toward the dumpster.

Moon reached into the dumpster and pulled out a bag. When he opened it, the aroma of fried chicken was strong. "I told you, man. We have our pick of the chicken they were selling just fifteen minutes ago."

Sam and Ziggy looked at each other for a moment and both shrugged. They each pulled a bag out of the dumpster and dug in. "I recommend staying away from the mashed potatoes, though," Ziggy advised.

23 ———————— April 28, 1969

Sam, Ziggy, and Moon rumbled down the dark road northeast of Independence, Missouri. Each took a piece of chicken, chomped the chicken off the bone, and threw the bone into the night.

"This place belongs to some friends of ours named Jerry and Ruth," Ziggy explained while waving another chicken leg. "They came back here from California and moved into Ruth's family farm after her parents died. They told us we could crash here awhile."

The night was warm, and the Volkswagen minibus had slowed down enough to be able to crack open all of the windows to their maximum. Flying insects swarmed in the headlights, some paying the ultimate price against the windshield. Sam felt they were soaring through the night in a biplane. Although it was hard to choose a favorite ride so far, Sam thought the exotic minibus might just be up there.

He looked forward through Moon's open windshield and saw an orange-red glow to the right of the road. As they drove closer, the glow transformed into a giant bonfire, with flames erupting at least ten feet high. They drove onto the gravel driveway. Almost as soon as they reached it, Moon jumped out of the minibus and opened a livestock gate to allow the bus access and then closed it when they passed. Cars and trucks of every description but "new" were parked haphazardly to the left of them. The bonfire was on the right, illuminating a white farmhouse with a large porch that was lit in the fire's glow. Ziggy parked the minibus on the left side of the driveway.

They walked into the sphere of light around the bonfire. A crowd of men and women in all states of dress and undress were swaying in unison as they sang "I-Feel-Like-I'm-Fixin'-to-Die Rag" by Country Joe and the Fish.

At least twenty dogs ran wild and free around the farm, exploring what they could. A big hound dog was laying on the front porch. He was content to observe the festivities until another large dog just off the porch committed some type of infraction. The hound dog growled and leaped off the porch at the offending animal, who quickly ran away. The hound dog returned to his post on the porch and lay down as if nothing had happened.

A couple approached them with open arms. Moon hugged the woman, and they shuffled back and forth in a small dance. Ziggy embraced the man, and they both patted each other's backs.

Ziggy backed away from the embrace and said, "Ruth, Jerry, this is Sam. Sam, Ruth and Jerry."

Sam started to put his hand out to Ruth, but she rushed in and embraced him. Ruth was full bodied and of medium height. Her straight black hair fell past her shoulders, which were covered in a long cotton work dress. She had wise blue eyes and well-defined smile lines around her mouth. Her big, genuine smile caused Sam's own.

Ruth said, "Welcome to our farm. We're really glad you could come."

Jerry, on the other hand, was tall and broad. His long, straight brown hair was tied into a long ponytail in the back, and his full beard tapered just below his chin. A worn, but dressy, blue oxford shirt was tucked into his ragged blue jeans.

Jerry gently slapped Sam on the back. "Come closer to our tribal fire, all of you."

Sam could hear a guitar, flute, and some percussion instruments. If there was a tune, he did not recognize it.

Jerry said, "Our farm has become a little like a way station for brothers and sisters traveling across the country. After they rest up and recharge, they get back on the road. Some people pitch in and help out by bringing food or whatever other ways they can."

Sam wished they had saved some chicken.

"People can stay as long as they want, as long as they behave themselves," said Ruth. "Well, sorta behave themselves."

The crowd contained people of every shape and size. There were whites, blacks, Asians, and Hispanics, roughly half men and half women. While he felt he was still the hair freak, the other men's hair ranged from slightly longer than his to extensive.

"Brothers and sisters!" shouted Jerry, turning toward the crowd and raising his arms.

Pointing to each of them, he said, "This is Ziggy, Moon Daddy, and Sam. They have just come from the wild west."

"You can call me Moon for short," said Moon.

The crowd approached them. Everyone milled around and took turns hugging each of them. Some of the women seemed a little more than friendly, and some were scantily dressed and sweating from their dancing around the fire. Sam couldn't help but wonder if this could be a buildup to a free-love experience, which he had heard a bit about. He had to admit that before Cheryl, this was the subject of more than a few of his fantasies. He decided to take a wait-and-see approach. In his ex-monk condition, his mind and body were always under marginal control and not completely trustworthy, so it would be safer to show a little restraint.

At least this was Sam's attitude until he had smoked half a joint and drank a half-bottle of wine. Then he found every woman to be utterly gorgeous, alluring, and warm. The music of their laughter filled him. Moon offered to give him one of the magic mushrooms that he had brought to Jerry and Ruth. But Sam thought maybe two new drug experiences in one day might be a bit much, so he thanked Moon and declined. Besides, he did not want to screw up how he was feeling at the moment.

Jerry was sitting on the ground with a circle of people near the bonfire, holding court.

"Look around you, my brothers and sisters," he said just loud enough to be heard by all. "We come from many places, and we are all different in many ways. I see white people, black people, Mexicans, Chinese, Indians. I see long hair and short. I see short people and tall people, both fat and skinny. Why are we here together? What do we have in common? We all like bonfires? We all like drugs and alcohol? We all trying to score a mate?"

Jerry paused, waiting for his class to respond.

"All of the above," someone yelled in the back.

Jerry nodded and continued. "Of course, all those reasons are part of why we're together. But those aren't the important reasons. I think we're here together because we share a vision of what the world can become, and we're looking for ways to make that happen. This vision is about the love and understanding between us as living beings. To realize this vision, we must treat all living beings with the respect and understanding that is due to them, after learning all we can about them. And remember: we are not such hot shits ourselves, not better or more enlightened than any others around us. Every living thing has some good and some bad. To really know others will lead to us understanding them."

A man called out, "What if this other living thing is trying to kick your ass, or worse, eat you?" Sam couldn't tell if he was joking or not.

Jerry thought a moment, pondering. "Imagine coming upon a grizzly bear," he said and closed his eyes, as if imagining it himself. His voice was soft, yet Sam didn't have any trouble understanding him. "Now you're no rube, so you, of course, have bear-repellent spray and know more than enough about bear habits. You have respect for the bear and have studied the bear to understand him. You know to stay still where you are and not appear threatening nor threatened. So you try that.

"But the bear has stopped eating and is walking toward you." Jerry opened his eyes and stared at each member in turn, letting the fear of the situation envelope them. "You are more afraid of the bear than you are of almost any other creature. You tell yourself to not hate the bear and to certainly not hate all bears for it. He is a magnificent creature, not made less magnificent because he is coming at you. Of course, you can't think of all this 'cause you're terrified like never before. You can't talk yourself out of being scared shitless either. The bear starts running toward you, and you know it's time to act. You growl back at the bear, try to look big, and prepare to shoot the repellent. The bear keeps coming. When he is fifty feet away, you squeeze the repellent trigger . . ."

His voice had gotten louder dramatically, and he even paused for effect. The group inhaled together.

"And nothing. The spray didn't work," he said quietly.

The group groaned.

"So what does this situation show us?" asked Jerry.

Another man shouted, "That you should have brought a gun?"

Everyone laughed.

"You are right," Jerry said, pointing to the man in acknowledgment. "Having a gun might have been necessary in this case. It certainly would have been helpful. No one is saying we shouldn't do everything we can to protect ourselves. But a respect for, and a knowledge of, grizzlies would help ensure that you have more than a few weapons up your sleeve. Then you could start with the least lethal weapon and escalate things only if necessary. If all the weapons don't work out for you, well . . . that's the circle of life, man. Natural selection just did not select you."

The group laughed again.

"We naturally fear what we don't understand and hate what we fear," Jerry continued. Sam noticed everyone was leaning in, holding onto Jerry's every word. One man had an apple halfway to his mouth like he had forgotten to finish taking a bite. "You can fear the grizzly. That fear helps keep all of us alive. But don't hate the grizzly. By all means, don't hate all grizzlies just because this particular one is trying to bite your head off. In the same way, don't hate the Chinese, the Russians, the rednecks, you name them. You may have to defend yourself against one or some of them. But it is rarely all of them, nor is it an issue of pure good or pure evil. Once you better understand how their natures and experiences make them what they are, you can sometimes reduce your fear. And you can almost always prevent fear from becoming hate.

"For example, Russians have many times shown themselves to be prickly assholes. They are always trying to push our buttons and get a rise out of us. For some damn reason, the Russian government feels they must be belligerent with us and the rest of the world to appear strong. They seem to think they advance their cause by domination, not diplomacy. Why do they always want to fuck with us?

"We can't just be pushovers when the Russians overstep the rules of civilization. But it's important to remember where they have come from. They suffered invasions from Napoleon and then twice from the Germans. Many Russians died, and their country was devastated. If that was my history, I think I would be prickly too. Isn't it better to consider how their experiences shape their behavior than to just assume they are evil? I believe thinking without hate gives us more options in solving our problems. All creatures are flawed, including man. Our flaws are another way we are all connected."

Jerry paused. "Shoot, people can always evolve too. The Japanese and West Germans are our buddies now." Jerry pointed to Moon. "Moon's ancestors, the Vikings, used to be the bogeymen of Europe in medieval times. They were brutal. Now who is more peaceful and laid back than the Swedes, Danes, and Norwegians?"

"Right on!" yelled Moon, pumping his fist in support. "Go you, Scandinavians!"

The group started to talk to each other.

"I know, I know," said Jerry. "Easy for me to say," he shrugged. But he seemed content with how his sermon had gone, so he let his crowd disperse.

Sam wandered around the farmyard, mesmerized by the bonfire and the crowd flowing around it. Everyone wanted to hug and welcome him. An impromptu band had formed with a guitar, flute, violin, and single drum. They were playing something close to bluegrass music and were much more proficient than the earlier musicians. People danced and twirled around the bonfire.

He noticed a tall, slender woman with long blonde hair looking at him from across the flames. He walked toward her. "I'm Crystal," she said as soon as he got close enough. "I was just reading your vibrations. They're very strong." Her silver-blue eyes seemed to look inside his skull.

"No kidding," he said, trying to figure out what she meant. "I'm Sam."

"I am very adept at determining people's spirit animals," she said.

"Really. What does that mean?"

"American Indians taught us that we each have a kindred animal who is connected to us in a spiritual way. That animal affects how we perceive the world and helps form some of our characteristics." She gazed unblinkingly at him.

"So you're saying we sense things like those animals, then we act like them?"

"In a way, yes."

"Alright. What's yours?" he asked.

"I am a silver fox."

He did not doubt it. "Well, I hope my spirit animal isn't something like an armadillo," he said.

She laughed and reached toward him. "Give me your right hand."

"Sure thing," he said, holding out his hand.

With her left hand, she caressed the back of Sam's hand and sensuously stroked his palm with the fingernails of her other hand. He jerked as an instantaneous electric current flowed from his hand to his crotch.

"You feel that?" purred Crystal. "That is your chi, flowing into me."

He could think of other another explanation for what he was feeling. But he certainly didn't say so.

She closed her eyes. "Oh, I see something . . . I see a bird. It's fierce, with piercing eyes and a sharp beak . . . a hawk! No wait—a falcon!" He started to pull his hand back, but she gripped it tighter. "Wait. There's more. One of the falcon's wings is bent. He is trying to flap his other wing, but he cannot fly."

As the night progressed with more beer and marijuana, passion overcame Sam's slight aversion to witches. He and Cheryl had both decided that they needed to get on with their lives and date other people until they could be reunited. That, combined with the wine and pot, lowered his inhibitions. He pushed his guilt back.

He and Crystal ended up nestled in his sleeping bag just outside the ring of firelight. They had been engaged in serious necking for hours, pausing only to drink some beer and rewet their chapped lips. They explored each other with their hands and lips, yet somehow silently communicated that they did not want to go too far.

He did not think this was free love yet. Not unless free love was just like some of his fondly remembered dates at drive-in theatres during high school. Whatever was going on now, it was just fine with him.

24 ——————————— April 29, 1969

Sam awoke on a cool, crisp morning. There was little wind, and the sky was a deep blue. The smell of fresh grass in the fields dominated the air, accompanied by the smell of bacon and coffee. Crystal stretched and yawned next to him in the sleeping bag. While she was still very fetching, the bright and less-than-romantic sunlight, coupled with the sleeping bag wrestling, had taken their toll.

Sam was sure he looked even more like shit. There was a stale taste of beer in his mouth, and he was a little dizzy.

They got out of the sleeping bag and shuffled toward a clump of people while carrying his camping kitchen gear. Ruth was pouring coffee and supervising a group of other women frying eggs, bacon, and potatoes under an open tent. Sam piled all of it onto his plate while Crystal took some potatoes and bacon.

"Well, good morning!" Ruth greeted them, looking amused at their matchup. "How did you two sleep last night? Or did you?"

The lady stirring bacon smirked.

"It was beautiful. Just beautiful!" Crystal cooed.

Sam just smiled. He was willing to go along with that description.

Crystal and Sam took their food and coffee to sit on a small hill near the farmhouse. Sam sipped his coffee slowly.

"So tell me more about yourself," he said.

"Hmm, let's see. My father's a minister in Arizona," she answered. "My mom's a nurse. I had a quiet, uneventful childhood. My parents clearly loved me and my little brother, but my dad was pretty distant and not that affectionate."

"We have that in common," he said.

She nodded, pausing to nibble at her potatoes. "When I became a teenager, I followed the path of many preachers' kids and became a bit of a wild child. I went to every party I could find." Crystal paused to remember. "I have to say that I had too much to drink way too many times."

"I can relate to that too. Who can't?"

"No, I seriously had a problem," she replied, gazing with a faraway look in her eyes. "When I was seventeen, I started experimenting with drugs. It was all about having a good time. For a long while, only I knew I had a drug problem. I could function all right. My grades were OK. But life was beginning to be a blur, and I knew I had to change course. I started studying various philosophies and religions in a search for some meaning in my life. Eventually, I left home to see more of the world and hopefully find a greater purpose."

"And how is that going?"

"It's been a struggle," Crystal said in an honest voice. "I never went to college, so I've worked as a waitress and held a variety of other menial jobs. I've not been able to find a new home yet where I'm completely comfortable and can establish that new life I've been wanting to find. On the other hand, I've lived in some beautiful places and met some wonderful people."

She placed her hand on her chest, looked at him, and smiled.

"I do feel my spirit growing stronger, and I'm happier than I've ever been. I feel more in tune with the world around me. I can take things as they come now. I don't need to know the whole entire path to peace. I only need to know how to trust myself to know whether to go right or left at the next turn. I even became a vegetarian." She picked up a strip of bacon and bit off a piece. "Though I still love bacon."

"Well, none of us is perfect," he said, grinning down at her.

When pried, Sam briefly recounted his story—leaving out Cheryl, of course. He also left out his draft problems. He was sick of talking about it. Crystal listened intently, occasionally reaching out to hold his hand.

Even though nothing serious happened, Sam did feel some pangs of guilt over their night of heavy petting and sharing a sleeping bag, less than a week after leaving Cheryl. Cheryl and Sam agreed that while their love was strong, their circumstances were not. They also realized that their love would likely only last if they could manage to one day be reunited. They agreed to keep loving each other and to work toward that day as much as they could. But until then, they had to lead their lives. That included dating other people. Despite this agreement, he did not feel particularly honorable about it now.

He had always loved girls and been in relentless pursuit of them. He remembered trying to hold a girl's hand at the movies when he was barely eleven. But his two older sisters had beat the concept of respect for women into him from an early age. Now he truly believed in that respect and tried to practice it. He admitted he could be overenthusiastic in some make-out situations, but he knew the word "no" to be holy. This was all it took for him to immediately stop and rein it in. There could be no passion unless it was a shared one.

But like most boys, he was powerfully pulled by his hormones. He recalled a time in early high school when a girl named Sandy suggested he sneak into her bedroom at night. It made little difference to them that she was on the second floor or that her parents' bedroom was just down the hall from her bedroom. Sam showed up outside Sandy's window at one in the morning. He climbed to her window with his fingers and toes between the bricks and tapped on the glass.

As they were necking and trying to be quiet, there was a knock at her bedroom door. Her father called her name from the hall and then started to open the door. Sandy yelled for him to wait, while Sam dove into her closet. Her dad stepped in. "I thought I heard some noise," he said. "Are you OK?"

"I'm fine," Sandy answered. Sam was amazed how calm she sounded under the circumstances. He felt like his own heart was beating loud enough for her dad to hear it through the closet door.

Things might have gone fine for Sam, but Sandy's dad saw a dress on the floor and decided to hang it up. Despite Sandy exclaiming loudly that she would do it herself, he then opened the closet door, which was how he found Sam: cringing in the dark between her dresses and among her shoes and gazing up at him in horror. He sprang like a rabbit between her dad's legs, knocking him down as he headed for the bedroom window. Luckily, the window was still open, and he took the screen with him as he dove out headfirst and plummeted to the ground. Somehow, he did not break any bones and ran off into the woods, clutching his pants while Sandy's dad went looking for his gun. Sam ran several hundred yards and hid in the dark woods, swearing to never again let his passion stomp all over his reason.

He felt very lucky that Sandy's bedroom was almost pitch black that night. But he also remembered sweating under his collar as he met Sandy's father two weeks later, when Sandy "introduced" them. It took a lot of convincing from Sandy for Sam to believe he wouldn't be recognized. But just in case, he was still ready to bolt at any time.

After breakfast on the farm, Sam went with the men working out at the barn while Crystal joined the women working in the garden. He worked with two men, repairing fences in the pasture. Sam was invigorated by the physical labor that produced something tangible and useful for the farm. After working for several long hours, he helped fix the loose swinging doors to the hayloft, and soon after, offered to split wood.

Sam had worked several construction jobs in high school, so he did not feel tool-stupid around the other men. He moved a little awkwardly at first, working with tools for the first time in almost a year, but he quickly regained the muscle memory to move efficiently enough through a task. Easy talking and laughter filled the air. The teams operated smoothly. He felt the sense that he was part of the community.

Everyone broke for lunch, during which they were served Brunswick stew and sandwiches under the tent. Crystal was spooning the stew into everyone's bowls. When they locked eyes, they exchanged smiles, and she blew him a kiss.

He carried his lunch to a picnic table and sat across from Ziggy. "I've been wondering," said Sam. "How did you and Moon end up together doing what you're doing?"

"When I got back from Vietnam, I was a real mess," said Ziggy. "I was having nightmares and was always angry. Dark thoughts were all in my head. I got in fights and couldn't hold a job. I was into some heavy drugs and even thought about ending it all. I hated myself."

"I'm sorry," said Sam, unsure what else to say.

"Anyway, that's when I met Moon in Oregon. I don't know why he chose me as a friend, but he did, and he never gave up on me. I guess you could say he saved my life with his goofiness."

Sam laughed. "I can see how it's pretty hard to remain dark and pessimistic around Moon."

Moon joined them at the table with his lunch. "Well, if it isn't my fellow wandering compadres," he said. He took a deep breath. "Ahh, isn't this the life? Hard, honest work in the sunshine and sleeping under the stars in the moonshine. How great is this?" He bit into his sandwich. He chewed, swallowed, and finished it off with a large swig of water. "I think I could do this for a while."

Ziggy said, "Moon and I are going to stick around here for about a week. Jerry and Ruth said you're more than welcome to stick around too. Moon and I told them your story."

Sam thought for a moment. "God, I'd love to stay. These people are incredible, and it's been a total blast," he said, looking around at all of them. "I can't remember the last time I felt so welcome somewhere."

Moon grinned. "Especially from a tall, winsome blonde lady."

He hit Sam on the arm and Sam shrugged. But after a pause, Sam spoke again. "But you know the clock is ticking for me."

"I know, man," said Moon. "What a bummer!"

The three of them gazed over the sunlit fields and pastures. Sam saw men and women resting during the lunch break or engaged in quiet conversations. He wished more than anything he could join them in this life they were living.

"We'll run you to the highway before dinner, pilgrim," said Ziggy, looking at Sam while staring wistfully at the fields and patting Sam on the back. He seemed like he understood.

As Sam went back to work, he thought about what Ziggy had told him over lunch. Ziggy's experiences in Vietnam had damaged him, almost beyond repair. If you were forced by your circumstances to kill, what would that do to your soul? He could not understand how one of the Ten Commandments was "Thou shalt not kill" while other Bible stories gloried in the battles of the chosen people. He was sure the people of Jericho had a different viewpoint about things as their walls were falling down. He fervently hoped that he would never be part of this level of brutality.

After work stopped at the end of the day, Sam went to Jerry and Ruth. "I just wanted to thank you guys both so much for your hospitality," he said.

"You are more than welcome, Sam," said Jerry. "You really worked hard out there today, and we all really appreciate it. I know you're going through a difficult time. But you'll find your way. You keep the faith, brother."

They shook hands and then Jerry enveloped him in a bear hug.

"You can stay here any time," said Ruth, giving him a motherly hug.

Sam sought out Crystal. She was washing up at an outside hose after working in the garden. She was wearing cutoff jeans with a denim work shirt, her sleeves rolled to her upper arms. Her shirt was partially unbuttoned, showing a T-shirt underneath, and her long blonde hair was tied in a ponytail. Her face was flushed from the sun and outside work, but her eyes were still penetrating. She was beautiful.

"Crystal," he called out hesitantly. "Can we talk?"

She turned to him with concern in her eyes. "Sure, Sam." She stepped away from the hose and followed him over to the side, away from any prying ears.

"I wanted to tell you that I've decided I need to keep moving," he said.

She sighed. "Oh, Sam. Why do you have to leave?"

"I have to get back in school as soon as possible to stay out of the draft."

She nodded immediately and stepped up to Sam to hug him. It seemed that perhaps this part didn't require that much explanation after all.

"I would have discussed all of this with you last night, but we were not doing that much discussing," he continued, trying to pull off a smile.

She squeezed him tightly and then pulled back and smiled. "I know, Sam."

But he needed her to understand too. "Last night with you in the sleeping bag and waking up next to you were all very special to me. I wish I could hang around here and get to know you better."

Her eyes softened. "I do understand. Don't worry. It was special for me too. Guess I'll always be attracted to farms and bonfires now."

"Me too, probably," he answered with a light laugh.

He wished he could get Crystal's phone number and address, but she had neither. It was the natural condition for many young people who were in transition across the country. He was torn between his attraction to Crystal and his deeper love for Cheryl. He had a sudden realization that Crystal, like several of the others he had met on this trip, was disappearing from his life and that he would likely never see or hear from her again.

"So we pass in the night," she whispered in his ear as they embraced once more. "I'll always cherish ours, Sam."

She leaned in and kissed him deeply but briefly.

Ziggy and Moon were standing by the minibus, ready to leave. They were pointedly looking in any other direction but theirs to give them privacy, but when Sam glanced at them over Crystal's shoulder, he saw Moon give him a grin and thumbs up.

They could wait just one more moment. Still hugging Crystal, Sam said, "Take care, Crystal. Go have the best travels, silver fox."

She pulled away and held his head in both of her hands, staring brightly into his eyes. "Keep being a good man, Sam. And stay free for me, alright?"

They both turned and walked away. She stopped, turned back and called, "And Sam?"

He looked back.

"Don't worry, baby. Your falcon will fly soon," she said.

Sam stood on the entrance ramp to I-70, south of Independence, Missouri, at half past five in the evening. It was a warm, soft evening, approaching dusk. The air was still. It was the time of day when the light, inhaling breeze of day had paused and the night exhale had yet to begin.

He couldn't help but reminisce about his trip and the people he had met so far. On the road, his urge to connect with others seemed heightened. Moon Daddy and Ziggy had become tight friends in less than two days, and Crystal had been more than a breath of fresh air. Several of the others he had stumbled upon were people who Sam truly thought he could be great friends with if they ever got the chance to meet again.

A glistening white 1967 Cadillac Deville convertible, with the top down, rolled past him and pulled over. The interior of the Cadillac was enormous, luxuriously appointed in turquoise leather and chrome.

"My God!" said Sam to himself. "What a ride!"

As he approached the car, he saw that two men were shouting at each other and pulling on something between them. The driver was a short, muscular man, and the passenger was tall and bulky, his skin doughy and pale. Both appeared to be in their thirties. "Let go, Clark!" yelled the driver.

The driver managed to yank the object from Clark and throw it out the open back, where it fell at Sam's feet. The object was two attached wire frames about four feet long with clear cellophane stretched over them.

"Goddammit, I'm not giving up my wings, Eddie!" yelled Clark.

"C'mon," Eddie said. "Be reasonable. He needs a place to sit!"

While Clark mourned his lost wings, Eddie opened his door, came to the back of the long trunk, and opened it. The trunk was huge but nearly full. Sam threw his bag in. He noted a jumbled pile of garments in one corner of the trunk. They were brightly colored, satiny outfits trimmed in lace and gauze.

"Sorry, more of Clark's costumes. I'm Eddie. Eddie Baxter."

Eddie had mid-length wavy hair combed straight back. His hair appeared to be set in concrete. The wind had picked up slightly, but not a hair on Eddie's head moved in the breeze. A thin mustache grew over his mouth.

"I'm Sam Roberts."

They shook hands. Eddie closed the trunk and pointed to Clark. "And this is Clark Alexander. Clark, this is Sam."

Clark was huge. Even sitting up front, Sam could tell he was around six-and-a-half feet tall. His doughy body filled the seat. He had long, straight black hair, and his pudgy face was dotted with pimples and covered in makeup that did not quite match his skin color. His dark eyes were darkened even more by black mascara. Sam reached his hand toward Clark, but Clark was still pouting and ignored him. In a meek voice, Clark unintelligibly muttered his case about his wings.

Sam climbed into the back seat, and they rolled away. As they reached highway speed, the wind buffeted him in the open back seat. Shouting above the wind, Sam asked where they were going.

They were from Los Angeles, and when asked what they were doing, Sam came to find out they were exploring the country. Both worked in the movies. Eddie was a film editor and Clark was a set designer. They both grew up in the Los Angeles area and had worked in film since their early twenties. Clark even seemed to forget about his wings and joined in the conversation a little.

"Los Angeles is an unreal world, at least around Hollywood," Eddie was saying. "Southern California is all we really know. We want to see the real America."

"So, what's Hollywood like?" asked Sam.

Clark said, "It's the land of make-believe. Almost anything goes. But contrary to what you might think, Hollywood isn't that much more tolerant about homosexuality than the rest of the country. In the film industry, the recognized position is still that men should be men, and women should be women. All kinds of things happen behind closed doors, but strong masculinity is still the official stance for men in Hollywood, to the point that they can lose their jobs if they don't conform."

Eddie laughed. "So even Clark needs to keep a lid on it in order to survive in our world."

"But on this trip, we want to be ourselves," Clark said firmly.

Sam thought these guys might be out of their league in the Midwest. If Clark thought Hollywood was intolerant of homosexuality, wait until he experienced small-town Missouri.

"I know it's not as intense as what you guys experience," he said, "but I also feel like I don't fit in the real world just yet."

"Tell us about it," said Eddie.

"I actually just resigned from the Air Force Academy," said Sam.

Clark whistled. "Wow, the Air Force Academy. Now there's a place where I'm sure we don't fit in."

Sam said, "Well, neither did I. And now I'm up in the air about what to do next."

Eddie and Clark expressed their sympathies, saying how it was hard to make huge decisions like that. They advised Sam to just be himself. "You have to do what your heart tells you to do," said Eddie. "And sometimes your heart tells you to do something hard." Sam thought about Cheryl and nodded.

Clark said he was hungry for dinner. They left the highway and pulled into a truck stop at the Oak Grove exit. When they walked into the diner, Sam noticed that about half of the tables and booths were filled with truckers and other travelers. A sign read, SEAT YOURSELF. Walking across the dining room, Clark could not have been any more flamboyantly gay if he had worn his wings.

They slid into a booth and ordered cheeseburgers and malts. The waitress was professionally polite, but did not call anyone hon. Diners around them either ignored them or stared with hostility.

"You detect we're not very welcome here?" Clark muttered.

"No shit?" said Eddie.

"C'mon, guys. This can't be a surprise to you," said Sam, glancing around at their audience. This didn't make it right by any means, but surely they had to have had this sort of experience before and knew how to handle it?

"No, it's not a surprise," answered Clark. "But the big reason for this grand trip was to let it all hang out for a while."

"Well, I think you let the wrong thing hang out," said Eddie pointedly.

After eating, they paid their bills and left the diner. As they approached the back of the Cadillac, four large men stepped from the shadows. One of them was drunkenly stumbling into the others.

"Whattaya faggots doing here?" the stumbling one shouted.

"That's right, ya homos," another called out. "Don't you know you're not welcome here? Take that sissy Cadillac back to California where ya came from!"

One of the other men looked at his buddies. "I think we need to teach these queers that they need to stay out of Oak Grove. Whattaya think?"

Sam thought he should try the same approach he attempted earlier in his trip during his disaster of a car ride with Leonard. "Hey guys, we just wanted to stop for dinner. We're not hurting anybody."

"Well, it's high time somebody here gets hurt," said the first man.

The four men stepped toward them, one hitting his fist into his palm. Clark stepped forward in front of Sam and Eddie. He seemed to pull his soft bulk up into his chest and transform himself from a six-foot-six pudgy man into a powerful menace.

In a deep, commanding voice, he said, "Now hold on, boys. I want you to consider something. You think you could beat us in a fair fight?

You might be right. But while that's happening, I promise you I'll bounce at least one of your heads off a car bumper here."

He reached over and hit the Cadillac bumper with his fist. The bumper responded with a dull thud of flesh and bone hitting metal. "Believe me," he bellowed. "I'm the master of the cheap shot!"

He paused and glared at the men. They didn't appear so confident anymore. "So who wants to be the guy who wakes up in handcuffs with his nuts swelled up to the size of baseballs?" Clark shouted. He stared menacingly at the man who first spoke. He turned his head to glare at the others. "Well?"

The four men looked at each other for support and found none. They looked Clark over, and apparently, they couldn't rule out the possibility that at least one of them could be seriously hurt by this hulking monster. Sam wondered if maybe Clark's black mascara added to the effect in their favor. The men slowly faded back into the shadows of the alley next to the diner, still brave enough to shout some threats their way but no longer courageous enough to act on them.

"And don't come back!" roared Clark.

After they were gone, Eddie and Sam patted Clark on the back.

"Who the hell was that guy?" asked Sam, staring at Clark.

Eddie laughed. "Clark seems as gentle as a bunny rabbit. But around the studios, he's known as a real bad ass."

Clark shrugged and sank back into his normal posture. In his natural voice, he said, "I was just channeling Clint Eastwood."

26 ——————— April 29, 1969

Cheryl and her housemates, Laurie and Jane, were seated together at a table in a dance bar named Rosco's on the outskirts of Boulder. The band was playing The Rolling Stones' "Satisfaction" while they sipped from large mugs of beer.

Jane shouted over the music, "I'm glad you decided to leave the convent and join us, Cheryl."

Laurie joined in, "Seriously, if you had stayed in the house any longer, you were going to be swallowed up by the couch."

"You both are so funny," Cheryl said in a deadpan voice. "Look, I appreciate what you're doing, but I just don't feel that festive."

"We'll be festive for you," said Jane. "Besides, this dark, mysterious thing you have going is kinda sexy."

Except for attending classes, Cheryl had been cloistered at the house, nursing the misery from Sam's departure. She wasn't sleeping well, didn't feel like eating, and battled an aching sadness. She hadn't bothered with makeup, and her hair had recently been more tangled than it had been in a long time.

She had learned to accept seeing him only occasionally while he was at the academy. Now that he was heading east away from her and entering back into the world, Cheryl couldn't look forward to a time when they planned to get together. She was hurting like never before.

She was glad that Jane and Laurie had talked her into going out on the town. They both stood over her at the house while she brushed her hair, applied her makeup, and made sure she put fresh clothes on. They had even picked out the outfit. They had pushed her out the door without taking no for an answer.

Now in the bar, she was energized by the music and realized she was even smiling sometimes. What could it hurt to mix it up with society again? She needed to establish her new life, whatever that might be. She was at Rosco's to celebrate with her friends and to make new ones.

A man approached the table. He was about Cheryl's age, about six-foot-three, well-built, and handsome. His straight light-brown hair was parted in the middle and hung below his ears. He was tan and clean shaven.

He came behind Cheryl's chair and leaned down until his mouth was close to her ear. "My name is Justin," he said into her ear, just loud enough to be heard above the music. His breath brushed against her ear, causing her to shudder a little. "I could see from way across the room how beautiful you are. I just had to come and see if you would talk to me."

Cheryl blushed. Part of her was uncomfortable. Another part of her was thrilled. She tried to become dark and mysterious again, but she was afraid she had already blown that.

"May I?" Justin asked Cheryl, reaching for a vacant chair at the next table.

"Oh, what's the harm?" said Cheryl's inner voice. "I came here to meet new friends and that's what I'm doing, isn't it? Then again, that opening line of his wasn't exactly 'buddy-buddy.'"

"Sure," she finally answered. "My name is Cheryl, and these are my friends, Jane and Laurie."

"Glad to meet you all."

Justin shook each of their hands but paused a few beats while holding Cheryl's. His eyes stayed locked on hers. Although he sat next to her, he talked to all of them, asking questions, listening carefully, and engaging and appearing interested in each of them. Come to find out that Justin was also a student at the university. He was a junior in business school, and he was from upstate New York.

While it was clear that most of his attention was directed at Cheryl, she was glad he related to everyone and not just her. He was certainly gorgeous, yet he also seemed humble, his humor self-deprecating. She was having a great time, loving the music, and feeling warm inside. He made her feel beautiful. He ordered another round of beers for all of them. Jane and Laurie stood and went together to the bathroom.

"I've always wondered why you ladies go as a group to the bathroom," he said. "What do you all have stashed back there? Is that where you all keep the good stuff?"

She laughed. "I'm so sorry, but I am sworn to the sisterhood to never reveal that information."

They both laughed and drank. He reached across the table and took her hand.

"I'm so glad you're such an interesting lady . . . as well as stunningly beautiful," he said.

She felt a warmth spread from her hand across her body. With his other hand, Justin gently stroked Cheryl's arm from her wrist to her elbow. She shivered and imagined herself in his arms. God, she almost wanted to pursue this. No, she definitely did. He slid his chair closer to her and brought his face close to hers.

"I'd love it so much if you'd choose to come with me this evening," he said.

"Where would we go?" she asked.

"Anywhere you want to go. I have a few favorite spots to show you."

Cheryl could not remember feeling so conflicted. On the way to being dropped off on the road, Sam had told her that he hated to imagine her with someone else. But he also said he could not expect her to pine away like a spinster as he figured things out. It just showed Cheryl that her happiness was so important to him. She felt the same way. They reluctantly agreed that each should see other people.

She thought that someday soon she would be ready to step out with someone like Justin, but not yet. She pulled her hand away. "I'm happy you want to be with me. You make a great first impression. But I feel like

I'm here under false pretenses. I recently separated from my boyfriend, and I'm not really into this. I'm just not ready, and it's not right for me to pretend I am."

To her relief, he smiled. "Thank you for being honest. But don't feel like you need to be so noble on my account. Pretend away," he said, and she laughed. "No one has ever accused me of having great timing, but my offer still stands," he said shrugging. "If you ever change your mind and want to use me on the rebound, I don't think I'll mind being used."

"I think the worse timing is mine. I didn't intend to mislead you."

"You didn't mislead me. I just couldn't stay away." He paused. "But if romance is off the table, I would still love to be your friend."

"Thank you," she said genuinely. Not a lot of guys would have accepted this as graciously as he had.

He wrote his phone number on a napkin and passed it to her. He stood and kissed her hand. In return, she stood and kissed him on the cheek. After that, with a humble smile, he simply walked away.

Jane and Laurie walked to the table, hugging and laughing. They looked at the empty chair beside Cheryl, then at Cheryl. "What the hell!" shouted Laurie. "I thought you guys were getting on famously."

Cheryl shrugged.

"You know I love Sam almost as much as you do," Jane said, pointing to Justin's empty chair. "But come on! Seriously?"

Cheryl smiled wistfully and sipped her beer. She framed her face with her hair, hoping they wouldn't see herself fighting back tears. "I'm sorry I've been such a wet blanket, you guys," she said softly.

She saw them glance at each other out of the corner of her eye. "Don't apologize for that. We just ... we hate to see you hurting like this. We're just doing what we can to try and fix it, that's all," Jane said gently.

"I just couldn't yet though," Cheryl said, shaking her head, and her friends nodded in understanding. "Maybe later." Cheryl lowered her gaze onto the table and traced a wet beer-mug ring with her finger.

She shoved the napkin in her purse.

27 ——————————— April 29, 1969

The Deville rolled smoothly down I-70. Eddie and Clark had raised the car top as the temperature dropped with the sun. They were just twenty miles from Columbia, Missouri.

"So where can we drop you in Columbia, Sam?" asked Eddie.

"Anywhere convenient. I'm going to the SAE fraternity, where I'm visiting some friends."

Sam had just decided that he was going to stop in Columbia at the University of Missouri to gather paperwork to possibly enroll there. Living in-state, he certainly would pay less tuition. He doubted he would be able to get the money to go to an out-of-state school, whether by working or getting it from his parents. He knew this from experience. When he was accepted at USAFA, he was also accepted at Cornell and Stanford. But it was understood that tuition at those two schools were more than excessive, and furthermore, his applications for financial aid went unfulfilled. He never even visited either school.

Since the air force paid him to go to the academy, the choice seemed obvious at the time. Sam wished he could go back in time and warn his younger self to reconsider. If he had enrolled at any other school other than the academy, he would not be mired in the draft mess he was in now. He would be taking the required hours, trying to keep his grades up and his nose relatively clean.

But then again, he would not have reunited with Cheryl. Sam realized with an ache that they might not make it, but he would not have traded a moment with her for anything.

"We can drop you right at the fraternity," said Eddie. "It's no prob."

"Thanks," Sam said, staring out the window. Suddenly he was faced with the fact that his journey cross country was almost over. He was finally reaching a destination. Sam couldn't exactly label the feeling that came with that.

A half dozen of Sam's high school classmates had joined the SAE fraternity at Mizzou. Most were close buddies with whom he had grown up. He hoped his friends would be good for a bed for the night. With the relatively balmy spring weather, he wouldn't mind sleeping out, either. A hot shower would be welcome, though.

One of his close friends was Mark Matthews. Their friendship dated back to junior high school. The pair had not talked since both left Kirkwood, but Mark was always happy to see him and was always up for a good time.

Mark was a charmer and could talk him into anything. He had introduced Sam to most of the bad habits he now possessed. He had taught Sam how to smoke and drink in the golf course sand traps during their no-car days. Mark always exuded an atmosphere of affection and fun, so certainly he could be forgiven for being a bad role model.

Mark had a cousin named Walt who lived in Springfield, Illinois, who had also become a friend of Sam's. In his senior year, they urged Sam to take a train and meet them in Springfield for a weekend. They told him which train to take and said they would meet him when it arrived. They expounded on the good time they would have.

Early on a Friday morning, Sam's dad drove him to the magnificent Union Station with its Romanesque revival architecture and soaring tower in St. Louis. He walked through the cavernous main waiting area with its massive arches. He caught a train, and two hours later, arrived at the Springfield Union Station, a slightly less-grand Romanesque structure, but nevertheless still an imposing old building.

Mark and Walt were nowhere to be seen. After hours of waiting, Sam threw up his hands. He did not know Walt's phone number or address, so he had no way to hear if something had happened that had caused the delay. He left the station through the front entrance and walked out onto Madison Street in a foul mood. He watched cars for a few minutes, not really expecting to see them but just trying to come up with a game plan.

He was pissed off at Mark and Walt, but he wasn't going to waste his train fare. Springfield was the hometown of Abraham Lincoln, so it had to be lousy with historical tourism. He decided to check it out before he headed back.

There was an informational sign on the sidewalk, showing what there was to see within walking distance. He would head for the center of town. The hell with Mark and Walt.

Sam walked a half block east on Madison and then turned south on Sixth Street. It was a warm, sunny day with a light breeze, and Sam welcomed the chance to stretch his legs in such nice weather after the two-hour train ride. On the corner of Sixth and Washington Street, he came upon the Old State Capitol square.

He was just walking up to the front entrance when he saw them walking across the capitol lawn.

When he caught up, he couldn't stop himself from yelling.

"Mark. Walt. What the hell?! Where've you guys *been?*"

They jumped and turned to him, confusion etched on their faces. "What the hell are you doing here?" Mark asked.

"What the hell am I doing here? You guys invited me, you dumb shits!" Sam exclaimed roughly, pushing his fist in Mark's chest.

"What?" stammered Mark. He squinted in concentration, thinking. "Man, I must've been really hammered, 'cause I don't remember doing that."

Sam turned to Walt. "You were there too, Walt."

"Oh, I heard him say it, alright," Walt answered, shrugging. "But he's always saying shit."

In addition to blowing off that Sam was coming, Mark and Walt now somehow thought they would be in trouble with their parents if it was known Sam was there. Sam did not completely understand their reasoning, but perhaps it was because they had not first cleared his visiting with their parents. Mark and Walt formulated a plan. He could pass for a local during the day. But they believed they had to hide him out at night. Sam stayed in a friend's bedroom that night and in someone's backyard the next. He was fine sleeping out, honestly. The weather at least was good, and someone even snuck out some blankets and pillows. Sam's anger didn't take long to dissipate.

On Sunday they went to a picnic on the lake. When they arrived, one of Walt's friends informed them that a policeman had been by, asking about Sam. An all-points bulletin had been issued for him in Missouri and Illinois.

It turns out that Sam's parents had called Mark's parents to find out when his train was arriving. It quickly became clear that Mark's parents knew nothing about what they were talking about, so the police calls went out. The police were not that concerned, given that Sam had only been gone a few days, but they told his parents they would put feelers out.

Sam, Mark, and Walt left the picnic and drove in hushed dejection to Walt's house. They appeared before a family tribunal, where all three were sternly lectured by the family patriarch. Walt's dad escorted him in shameful silence to the train. Sam's dad picked him up at Union Station in St. Louis for yet another silent ride where the real lecture didn't start until he got home and had to face his parents together. He was grounded for a month. Neither his mom nor his dad bought his unlikely story. Maybe they just could not believe their son could be so stupid.

He was ready to kill Mark.

But he conceded that Mark had no malice and likely could not help himself. In fact, Mark had always showed a high regard for the welfare of others around him. Even so, Sam vowed to never trust him again. But the problem with Mark was that he was so convincing, and Sam would likely believe him again the next time he tried to pull Sam into one of his many adventures.

28 ———————————— April 29, 1969

The white Cadillac rolled up the driveway to the SAE House. The driveway was lined with large, white-painted stones. An old but shining white mansion rose from the top of the hill, its steps and columned porch illuminated with outside lights. Twin stone lions guarded the entrance sidewalk and steps while several young men came and went through the heavy wooden doors.

Clark said, "God, we could film *Gone with the Wind* here."

"You're right about that," said Eddie. "I can picture Scarlett O'Hara strolling through those doors, her gown covering the entire front porch."

"It's pretty overwhelming," Sam said. He had never visited the house either. The large white structure was imposing and a little intimidating. He reminded himself that it was only a bunch of guys like him inside.

Eddie added, "What do you bet, Clark? Do you think we'd be welcome to hang out here?"

"Yeah," Sam said. "Sorry about that. I'm afraid you're right. I'm sure there's an explosive concentration of male hormones in there. You would definitely need to keep your costumes hidden away if you didn't want to get your butt kicked, Clark." He paused. "I've seen you in action, though.

I think you could hold your own." Then he hesitated again. "Look, I had no right to question how you looked or acted at the diner back there. You deserve to be you, anywhere you go."

Eddie looked back at him appreciatively. "No prob. We both know you would have been slugging it out with us if it had come to that."

Sam clapped Eddie and Clark on the backs. "You know it. Thanks for the ride. You guys be careful."

Clark went back to open the trunk, and Sam removed his bag. He gave Clark a hug. Clark stiffened for a moment, then relaxed and hugged Sam back. Clark got back in the front seat, and they drove off from the house, all three waving.

Sam looked around to take in the house and grounds. It was a lush, spring night, and the ambience surrounding him was of the nightlife ready to get started. The fraternity house was at the top of its own gentle hill, the spacious front lawn stretched into the darkness at the bottom of it. From the hilltop, he could see lit campus buildings to the east.

Sam abandoned his bag in an empty, discreet place at the side of the house. He went inside the front door into a large entry hall and approached a student, inquiring about Mark.

"Hey, Billy," shouted the student to another student, "have you seen Mark Matthews?"

"I think he's upstairs," answered Billy. "I'll find him."

"OK. Thanks," Sam said and sat on a couch.

When he came down the stairs, Mark shouted in surprise. "Roberts!" he yelled, running toward Sam. They gave each other backslapping hugs.

"Where ya been, man?" Mark asked. Sam told Mark the condensed version of his saga, figuring details would come later, and asked if he could crash somewhere for the night in the house.

"I'm sure there's a bunk somewhere," answered Mark. "Here, let me show you around."

The main floor was tastefully furnished and decorated. The hardwood floors were polished to an unblemished sheen. The main floor contained an entrance hall, living room, and dining room—all spacious and spotlessly clean, thanks to the forced labor of the fraternity's pledges. Sam bet he could join a fraternity and put up with the pledge crap. After all, he had experienced even worse abuse as an academy grunt. And the fraternity probably didn't run them to death. Still, he was not eager to jump into another role as an abused lowlife.

Going upstairs, the décor was more industrial, appropriate for eighteen- to twenty-two-year-old men with questionable housekeeping skills. Each bedroom was wood paneled with built-in bunkbeds and desks, and each housed two men. Mark showed Sam one of the empty rooms.

Mark said, "You're welcome to crash here. Why don't you clean up, and we'll meet on the hill in front of the house in an hour? Some of us are driving over to Cosmo Park to meet some girls there."

After dragging his bag to the room, Sam showered, shaved, and rummaged through Edna's laundry for some suitable civilian clothes.

Sam and Mark rode through the night in Mark's Ford Falcon. Two of their old friends from high school, Phil and Steve, were riding in the back.

"It's Tuesday night," said Sam. "How can you party like this when you've got classes tomorrow?"

Mark grinned, tapping his thumb on the steering wheel to the beat of the song playing. "I only have one class on Wednesday, and I don't have to be particularly conscious to attend."

"Around here, there isn't a lot of difference between weekdays and weekends," added Paul. "There's always some trouble to get into."

"The tricky part is learning to say no before your grades go in the shitter," said Steve, raising his sunglasses that he had worn despite the time and giving Sam a pointed look.

"That's right," said Mark. "I'm getting about a C– in saying no."

Cosmo Park was the nickname for Columbia Cosmopolitan Recreation Area. There was a golf course, which wove around lakes, ballfields, playgrounds, and picnic areas. They drove to an open area close to one of the playgrounds. The open area was bordered by trees, which somewhat shielded it from the main road.

Sam saw there was already a good crowd. All were sipping beer or punch from plastic beer glasses. Conversation and laughter filled the air. He surveyed the gathering and saw several beautiful coeds scattered throughout the crowd. Compared to Boulder, the people dressed a little more conservatively, though there were the occasional hippies. A car's doors were opened, and its stereo was playing Iron Butterfly's "In-a-Gadda-Da-Vida."

Mark led Sam to the beer keg, which was hidden under a tarp. A metal washtub, filled with something resembling punch and ice, was also hidden underneath. A bucket near the keg asked for reimbursement money.

"That's the secret weapon," said Mark, pointing to the punch. "It's mixed with a grain alcohol called Everclear. Tastes great and will knock you on your ass."

Sam tasted the punch and liked it. He finished the glass, but then switched to beer. He did not want to flame out early.

Mark shouted a greeting to a girl named Beth and gave her a hug when they reached her. He introduced Sam, and Beth introduced her roommate, Janelle, a girl with dark brown hair and warm eyes to match.

"Very glad to meet you, Janelle. Hello, Beth," said Sam politely, shaking their hands.

The four of them meandered through the crowd. They appeared to have had arrived late as the rest of the gathering looked like they had had a head start on the festivities.

One group was playing a game resembling tag near the woods. As Sam watched, the person who was "it" chased another young man. Both ran at top speed, and the pursued man was looking back at his pursuer and laughing. Then the chased man turned his head back ahead and accelerated. He rammed full speed into the trunk of a large oak tree, bounced off, and crashed to the ground. The pursuer laughed but then must have seen room for concern because he quickly ran to him to make sure he was alright. The crowd was silent. As his friends gathered around the fallen, the crowd murmured their concern.

After a minute, the man staggered to his feet and raised both fists in the air. He bounced up and down victoriously. Everyone cheered and raised their glasses in response.

"See what we do to entertain our guests?" Janelle said and laughed.

"I'm impressed," Sam answered. "Does the night end with a demolition derby of our cars too?"

"Now that's an idea!" she said.

Sam turned to Mark. "How can you party like this in a city park? Isn't it closed?"

"Nah, Cosmo Park is never closed. It seems like the police don't pay a lot of attention to you unless you are committing some kind of mayhem. So far, we play it cool, and they do too."

"We keep the music down and try to hide behind the trees. No one's been hurt as far as I know. So far not too badly, anyways," Beth added, glancing over at the guy who had crashed face-first into a tree.

"We love this park," said Janelle. "We'd never do anything to harm it."

The four of them continued to mix with the crowd. Sam and Janelle talked about where they were from, what they were studying, and what they wanted to do with their lives. He spoke to almost everyone at some point. The conversation was somewhat light and superficial, but everyone was warm and friendly enough, so this didn't bother Sam much. It seemed that as soon as he would finish his drink, Mark would grab him to go back for another round. With each one, conversations seemed to become more and more fascinating and humorous. Sam couldn't help but notice that, with every drink, Janelle was becoming even prettier. If he was the first one to laugh at her jokes and the last one to stop, he didn't notice.

Sam awoke on top of a picnic table in the bright midmorning sun to the sounds of children playing. His eyeballs hurt as he looked around and noticed that the table was about ten feet from a playground. Preschool children were playing all around him and shouting, making his head throb. Several teachers were eyeing him suspiciously.

"Miss Peggy," called out a little girl near him. "Is there something wrong with that man?"

As one of the teachers pulled the little girl away from him, Sam's voice cracked as he sat up and spoke. "Sorry, you guys. I was just taking a little nap, that's all."

He pushed himself off the table and backed away from the kids and teachers, his hands raised up in mock surrender. He saw they were backing away from him too, the teachers pulling the curious children away with them.

"Excuse me," he mumbled to any other lingering kids as he crossed the playground to exit as quickly as he could.

Once he felt he had cleared the imagined expulsion zone, he ran.

"Why do I always fall for your shit, Mark?" he said aloud. But he had to admit that from what he could recall, it was a good time all around.

29 ————————— April 30, 1969

Sam walked the three-and-a-half miles back to the Mizzou campus. He found himself at Francis Quadrangle, the oldest part of the Missouri campus. He saw an open, rectangular green field lined with stately limestone-trimmed brick buildings. Large trees lined the edges of the open field and were clustered among the buildings, shading the walkways and courtyards. To the left, Sam saw six high stone columns standing together in the open field, like ancient druid monuments. The sharp aroma of freshly cut grass added to the parklike feeling of the place.

The morning had warmed, and he heard songbirds in the trees. Young men and women strolled around in the sunshine or hurried to their next classes, weighed down with textbooks and bags. Many of the girls wore short-shorts, and he could not help admiring their long, slim, tan legs.

Sam walked up to a large nine-story domed building called Jesse Hall. He entered, walked up to a directory in the cavernous entrance hall under the lofty ceiling and found the registrar's office listed on the second floor. A large daunting sign, which listed all the colleges at the university, rose high above him. The choices were endless ... and they were choices

Sam needed to make. He was nervous about making another bad choice in his college career. He told himself that he didn't necessarily need to figure out the rest of his life right now. Right now, he just needed to get into school.

Limestone steps led to the second floor. The steps were worn down in the middle after almost a century of students climbing and descending them. All along the upstairs hallways were the administrative offices. Voices echoed throughout the expansive halls.

He walked into the registrar's office and asked for a course catalogue and enrollment forms. He took them to a nearby table and started to flip through them. The summer schedule was not yet released, so it was too early to pick specific classes. He just needed to fill out and submit the application forms to be considered for enrollment.

One form required him to declare a major. His major was engineering at the academy, but so was practically everyone else's. He was unsure if the economy still favored engineers. There were stories of aeronautical engineers selling hot dogs in Seattle after aircraft manufacturing layoffs. The problem was that he did not know what he wanted to study next if not engineering. Of course, it was possible to change his major later if he did not like it. With this thought to comfort him, he chose the College of Arts and Science, since he knew many fields of study started with this anyway.

He finished his paperwork and gave the package to a clerk. He was, despite some other lingering feelings of overall anxiety, confident that he would be accepted. He also knew that despite his turmoil at the academy, his academic credentials were still strong. How to pay for it was another matter. He pushed that thought to the back of his mind. He could do nothing about it right then.

He left Jesse Hall and continued to stroll the campus, soaking up the feeling of the knowledge and freedom that he hoped to attain. All the students he saw were happy and not afraid to look Sam in the eye when they passed. Most even nodded at him.

Downtown Columbia was only a few blocks from campus with shops, bakeries, and restaurants lining Broadway. At one point, he sampled homemade banana bread with dark Italian coffee, which he sipped at as he browsed. Ambling through the shops, he pawed over keepsakes before finally settling on a Mizzou T-shirt. Certainly now was the time to do such things. At about midway through his day, he ordered a Reuben sandwich and an iced tea for lunch at a sidewalk cafe. Contentedly savoring it, he listened to the conversation and laughter around him. Like Boulder, Columbia was a young, vibrant college town with an atmosphere of both good times and serious study.

"Unlike Boulder," he said to himself, "Cheryl isn't here."

Sam was hit with a sudden pang of longing. He yearned for the sound of her voice. Sam quickly found the nearest pay phone and called her.

"Cheryl?" Sam asked hopefully as soon as the other end picked up.

But it wasn't Cheryl's voice that greeted him. Sam instead recognized the voice of Jane, her housemate. "No, she's in class," Jane answered. "Who's this?"

"It's Sam. Please tell her I called, okay? Tell her I'm in Columbia, Missouri." There was a moment of silence on the other end.

"I sure will, Sam."

"And please tell her I love her."

"Absolutely."

As he was walking to the SAE house to get his bag, Sam thought how even though Columbia wasn't Boulder, it was not a bad plan B. He really was animated at the prospect of being at Mizzou. He just needed one more person there with him to make it perfect.

Sam stood at the end of the I-70 entrance ramp just northeast of Columbia. He had said goodbye to everyone just before, but he was now regretting not staying just a bit longer. Dark clouds were building in the west. The temperature had decreased to the mid-fifties, as evening and another weather front approached. Sam was on the last leg of his journey.

He felt satisfied and responsible enough to have submitted his application to Mizzou. At least he had done something to resist getting drafted, rather than just fretting about what to do. It was a small step, and Sam knew his troubles were not even close to over, but merely having a definite direction for plowing ahead gave him relief for now.

He observed the thick black clouds approaching, towering a thousand feet above him, and Sam could feel the air become still. There was a pale-green cast to the evening light. The green-light phenomenon was more common in the Midwest than other regions in the US and usually happened before tornadoes or other severe thunderstorms. Despite the still air around him, Sam could hear a roar to the west, like a huge waterfall in the distance. The roar's volume started low but rapidly increased as its source grew closer.

He saw a low, even blacker wall about a half-mile away at the base of the towering thunderheads. As the wall approached, he saw branches and other debris blowing around in the dark gray barrier. He could not see anything beyond. The roar became deafening. He knew he had to get out of the open and find some cover.

He looked around for anything that could be used as shelter. He was surrounded by a large meadow and saw that the nearest woods were too far away to reach in time. He threw his bag into a roadside ditch and dove in next to it. He found his shovel in his bag and frantically dug a small shallow hole that might offer some protection. He lay in it and pulled the dirt and bag over him as best as he could just as the wall of wind hit.

He felt the force of both the wind and rain as a physical presence, pushing at him from all sides. He held tightly to his bag with both hands. It felt like the weight of it was all that was holding him down. His head being under the bag didn't stop him from hearing the peppering of debris on the canvas, loud enough to be heard above the howl of the wind. He heard and felt even larger flying objects bouncing off the bag. He didn't even want to know what they were. Even more terrifying was the idea of the wind swallowing him up, or perhaps that something heavy would take him out right then and there. Ten minutes of terror later, the wind diminished. Sam could hear the roar receding to the east. He felt that the temperature had dropped at least ten degrees. As if that was not enough, the wind was replaced by a heavy downpour.

He pulled his rain poncho out of his bag and put it on. He dug his hole deeper and wider, creating more room for him and his bag. He sat there and spread his poncho over the gap. Ducking his head inside the poncho's head opening, he drew the string on the hood to close it tight. He relaxed a little, thinking that perhaps now he would stay dry.

But he was also getting cold. He pulled out a small flashlight from a side compartment on his bag and rummaged through the rest of his contents as the rain pelted the outside of the poncho. He put on extra shirts and sweaters to little avail. He finally pulled out his sleeping bag and crawled inside it.

Fifteen minutes later, Sam started to warm up. He was relatively snug and felt secure in his makeshift habitat despite the hard rain continuing. All in all, he thought that he had done a pretty decent job of riding out the storm. He was dry and, for the most part, warm. Now that the fear was subsiding, he was almost sleepy.

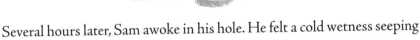

Several hours later, Sam awoke in his hole. He felt a cold wetness seeping into his jeans. The downpour had changed to a light, cold rain. He saw and heard water beginning to flow in the ditch and realized his hole was starting to fill up, soaking his sleeping bag. He tried to tuck the bottom of the poncho under him, but the water kept running around it and continued to seep into his sleeping bag and jeans.

He got out of the sleeping bag and poked his head back through the poncho opening to assess the damage. As he stood up and climbed out of his hole, he tried to drag his duffel bag out of the ditch to spare it from more water, but there was no use. The duffel bag, sleeping bag, and peacoat were already soaked. He felt the cold spreading over other parts of his body. As he started pacing on the roadway trying to stay warm, his mind raced through possible methods to survive the night. He explored every plan and action he could think of, but he kept running into walls in his mind.

The temperature had dropped to the mid-forties when the front came through. Sam thought about his survival training. He was not afraid of the temperature alone, but combining that temperature with being wet was a different matter. His pacing would help keep him warmer, but the cold and wet could cause hypothermia or rapid body-heat loss, even with a temperature in the fifties. And it was ten degrees colder than that. He thought about digging into the earth and covering himself with dirt for insulation, but that would not help when the dirt was mud.

He continued pacing through the night, shivering uncontrollably. The rain had stopped, and there were stars in the cold sky. When predawn arrived, Sam felt like the temperature was in the thirties, but he had no way to know in his present condition. Time stretched out, and each moment brought more suffering. His entire body was numb. All other thoughts were pushed from his head by the cold that gripped his bones. He quoted air force trivia in his head as a distraction. What was the top speed of the F-4? How high could a B-52 fly? What were the words to the Air Force Academy motto?

In time, the eastern sky lit up in bright oranges and pinks. As the sun rose, Sam shakily sought out its rays for the small amount of heat he could gain from them. He could now fully assess the damage the storm had caused. Branches and other debris were everywhere, including the road. He saw many pieces broad enough to have seriously hurt or killed him had he been struck with them. There were no cars. He kept pacing. He prayed for a break from his misery, promising to live a better life if God would help him.

30 —————————————— May 1, 1969

A large, green pickup truck was driving slowly toward him on I-70. The truck was maneuvering around tree branches, pieces of billboards, and other debris that littered the road. The truck had to stop several times for the driver, a large black man, to be able to get out and drag some branches out of the way. Sam wondered why the roadcrews had not been out yet. He could only figure they were elsewhere, dealing with more serious damage. When the truck stopped near him, the driver again got out of the truck. He pulled a branch aside and looked at Sam.

"You all right, man?" the driver asked.

Sam shuffled closer to the driver. "I'm alive is about all I can say. I was stuck here all night."

The driver looked impressed and whistled. "Wow, you were here when the storm hit?"

Sam nodded.

"Well, you get in the truck, and we'll get you warm."

Sam tried to lift his wet bag into the back of the truck, but he lacked the strength. Luckily, the driver was kind enough to help him. The heat—

once they both climbed into the front of the truck—was heavenly, and Sam thanked God for his rescue. His skin was starting to regain feeling, and he felt the pinpricks in his warming ears and nose. He held out his hand.

"My name is Sam. Thank God you stopped. I don't know how much longer I could have taken it."

"My name is Wilson Roberts," said the driver, taking Sam's hand.

Sam said, "Wow, my last name is Roberts too."

"Pretty cosmic!" Wilson said and laughed. "Wanna bet we're long-lost brothers?"

Wilson was a large, muscular man in his mid to late thirties. His dense hair was cropped into a neat workingman's Afro haircut. His dark brown face was clean shaven, and he was dressed in work clothes.

"What was it like out here?" asked Wilson. "I felt lucky I was safe at home, but it was pretty scary there too."

Sam said, "I've been in hurricanes, and that storm was just as bad. Maybe worse. It came out of the blue like some swirling black wall. I was flat on the ground when it went over. Was it a tornado?"

"No, they're saying it was just a severe thunderstorm. The weatherman said it was straight-line winds, caused by a very, very high-pressure front ramming into a very, very low-pressure one or something like that. The winds were over ninety miles per hour, so it did a lot of damage. The temperature dropped about fifteen degrees in no time, and the air pressure dropped so fast that most of the back windows on cars blew out. My truck was saved, for some reason. Some big old trees were blown over, sometimes pulling whole yards up."

"I can believe it. Hope you made it through all right," said Sam. "Any family?"

"We came through OK. A lot of debris is all. Thanks for asking. Yeah, I have a wife and two kids—a boy and a girl."

"That's great," Sam said and paused. "There're no cars out here with this shit blown everywhere. What're you doing out on the road anyways?"

"Have to catch a train in St. Louis this afternoon. I'm a flagman for the Union Pacific Railroad. I have no choice but to get out here and battle whatever Mother Nature has to offer. I have a chainsaw in the back if I need it. I'm riding a caboose back to Kansas City. I don't ride, I lose money." He shrugged.

"Well, thanks for coming by. I'm grateful," said Sam.

Pointing at the floor, Wilson said, "There's coffee in that thermos and a cup in the glove compartment. Help yourself."

Sam poured a cup and sipped it, marveling over the delicious combination of desperation and strong, hot coffee. He warmed his hands on the cup, feeling them start to tingle comfortingly with the warmth.

Wilson continued to drive slowly down the highway, weaving around the debris. When their route was completely blocked by branches, Sam got out to help drag them out of the way. In a few miles, the road was clear enough to speed up a bit.

"How'd you become a flagman, Wilson?"

"The railroad has always been a big part of my life," Wilson replied. "My dad was a porter, so I guess it's in my blood. For me, it's a good job." Sam nodded. Besides battling Mother Nature as Wilson put it, Sam could see it being a neat job too.

"But where are you heading that you ended up wandering around in a storm of biblical proportions anyways?" Wilson asked.

"St. Louis," Sam said. "I was in Columbia to see some friends and check out the school. Other than that, let's just say I'm between jobs."

"OK, let's say that," Wilson replied, and luckily he seemed to be content leaving it at that, leaning over and turning up the radio. The Isley Brothers sang "It's Your Thing" as they moved to the music.

When the song ended, the news began, one story speaking of an ongoing trial of a Black Panther group called Panther 21, who had been indicted for planting bombs at three locations.

"What a mess!" said Wilson, shaking his head as they drove along.

After a pause, Sam squirmed. He wasn't sure what was easier: changing subjects or adding to the one that hung heavy in the air. He finally decided. "I don't know if you're comfortable talking about racial politics."

Wilson also paused. "When it comes to race," he said, "we're all hesitant to discuss it and equally hesitant not to discuss it."

"OK. Let's try," said Sam. "What do you think of the Black Panthers?"

Wilson ran his hand through his hair. "I don't like a lot of their methods. But they do some good things too, like food drives and education and stuff. They're also spewing out anger and hate, which I don't appreciate. But I understand their anger. Hell, I'm also angry about the shit I see all around. Can you imagine what it's like to always be looked at with disdain or fear? Do I look like a deadbeat or a criminal to you?"

"No, sir."

"I still feel that fear," said Wilson, "whenever it's the police or a big white crowd. My heart races, and the hair stands on the back of my neck. Now that I'm a parent, I'm really afraid for my children and their future."

Sam let his words hang for a bit before speaking. "I'm already afraid enough when I see blue lights in the rearview mirror. But I think I'm more worried about getting in trouble, not getting hurt. I can't imagine how intense it would be to fear for your life during it." He paused. "I grew up in an integrated town. We knew each other, and I don't remember ever feeling fear or disdain from the black people there. But I guess I'm still uncomfortable around black people I don't know, though. I can almost feel the hostility and doubt. Just the idea of not knowing."

"Have you ever been arrested for just hanging around somewhere?" asked Wilson, glancing over at him. "Have you feared that you would be beaten or killed when that happened?"

"I've been arrested, but I've never feared that I'd be beaten or killed," Sam admitted.

"Well, I have," Wilson said. "It's a terrifying experience."

Sam was sure that Wilson would not have received a pat on the head and a "You go home now and be careful" from the cops who may have stopped him. As they drove, Wilson told him that today's black men and women had much to be pissed off about, and rightfully so. They talked about how black people were still fighting the abominations of Jim Crow laws and segregation, even a hundred years after the end of slavery. Civil rights legislation had recently been passed, but southern states were either ignoring those laws or finding work arounds to discriminate just the same. Even in most of the northern states, there was inequality in housing, employment, economics, education, and other critical components of life. Sam imagined that the fear and anger stemming from experiencing injustice and the frustration of being denied the tools for a better life had to be overwhelming.

Sam was brought back from his thoughts by Wilson who spoke again. "A black man is twice as likely to fight in Vietnam or be jailed than a white man. He's not likely to be sheltered from the draft in some college. Or he might enlist because he sees no other good work opportunities. In short, we black men are sick and tired of being considered less than human, and it makes us angry. We look around us and see white people feeling entitled and superior. My momma taught me that there is a definite line between feeling proud and fortunate about your situation and feeling privileged and entitled to it."

"I can see that," said Sam.

Wilson spoke with intensity and anger, but his deep, calm, and friendly voice assured Sam that he was not the target of any of it. He did feel fortunate that he was not raised under the specter of poverty and that he was able to attend good schools. Talented and enthusiastic teachers had made classes at least mildly interesting. They had lit a love of learning and had prepared him well. He didn't like to think that a good bit of his good fortune may have come at a cost paid by others who were less fortunate. He certainly didn't feel entitled to what he had received.

Sam continued, "When you picked me up, wouldn't it have been great if neither of us thought about skin color? We could have looked into each other's eyes and sized each other up based on what we saw there."

"Sounds pretty sweet," said Wilson. "We don't seem to be moving very fast in that direction though. What I would love to see in the near term is that, for once, we recognize and embrace those differences."

"Maybe it'll take an invasion from Mars for us to realize we're all human," said Sam.

They laughed.

Sam spoke up.

"When I was thirteen or fourteen," he said, "I used to go to the city park during the school year and find pickup football games. There were large gatherings of white kids and black kids, and we all played pretty easily with each other. I had some good black friends too. The games stopped in the summer though. I went to my white world, and they went to their black one. I remember when we came back to play after summer vacation in 1964, things had changed. I don't remember any fights or open hostilities, but I felt this new level of unease and suspicion. After a few awkward starts, the pickup games just sort of evaporated."

"That's too bad. Why do you think that happened?" Wilson asked.

Sam had a pretty good idea. The summer of '64 was pretty eventful to say the least in regards to the changing of civil rights. The Civil Rights Act was signed into law at about the same time three civil rights workers were murdered in Mississippi. That summer also saw race riots in Harlem, Rochester, and Philadelphia.

Sam could only shake his head, remembering several of the kids that he had once thought the world of. He wished he could remember some of their names. "All of us kids were coming to an age when we started paying more attention to the events around us, I guess. But I also think that all of us young boys were passing from adolescence to young manhood, so that innocence of childhood was disappearing, you know? Maybe our hormones were in overdrive. I don't know. In any case, we stopped seeing each other as friends."

"That is sad," said Wilson. "What you say makes sense to me."

Wilson and Sam looked out the windows and thought silently.

"Well, we can be friends and maybe turn this tide the other way," said Wilson, holding out his hand. "This has to be solved between individual people before we can solve it as a society, wouldn't you say?"

Sam shook Wilson's hand. He sensed a level of empathy and understanding with Wilson that could not have been more of a contrast to what he sensed with Leonard.

"I'd be honored," said Sam.

31 ——————————— May 1, 1969

Sam and Wilson rode in the truck on the US-40 bridge across the Missouri River. The river was running high and wide. Sam noticed that the water was muddy, the color of chocolate milk. As they crossed into St. Louis County from St. Charles County, the land changed from low river bluffs on the St. Charles side to a flat, open floodplain in St. Louis County. Passing through the town of Gumbo, he saw very little but bare fields, a few low buildings, and a prison. As they drove on, Sam told Wilson about his current situation and his uneasiness over going home.

"We 'bout there?" asked Wilson.

"Pretty close. Kirkwood is just a little southeast of us."

Wilson said, "Have you given any thought about what you're going to say when you see your folks?"

Sam sighed. "I think about it all the time. I've gotten a lot of anguished phone calls and received even more letters since I resigned, so I have an inkling on how it will go. My mom doesn't like it, but she is at least a little sympathetic. But my dad . . . he's taken a very hard stance."

"Why's that?" asked Wilson.

"'Cause that's who he is, I guess," answered Sam. "Look, I get how he's all disappointed. He went to Texas A&M, which was a military school—even more so when he went there. He served in the war and had a great career as an officer. I guess he dreamed the same for me."

"It's good that you can see that. But you gotta live your own dreams, not his. Right?"

"Yeah, I agree. But try telling my dad that. I've tried myself, but it's never ended well. I don't expect anything but hostility from him over this."

They rode on in silence.

"Who knows? Maybe things will change," Sam said. "But in the meantime, I just need to work on not letting him affect me that much. Guess it's time to find my support elsewhere."

"I don't know the man," said Wilson, "but maybe it's his love for you that's making him so adamant about things. He may be convinced that his way is the best for you too. And he only wants what's best for you. Believe me, I'm a father, and I can relate."

"Well, I guess that's a little comforting," Sam said.

Sam and Wilson rolled to a stop in front of Sam's parents' house. He no longer thought of it as his house. Wilson wrote his name and phone number on a piece of paper and gave it to Sam.

Wilson said, "You better give me a call the next time you're in Columbia. You can meet the family."

Sam reached over with both hands and grabbed Wilson's hand. "I'll be in touch. You saved my ass, Wilson. I owe you."

They got out of the truck and wrestled with Sam's sodden, heavy bag, throwing it on the driveway.

"Your mom is going to love that load of laundry," Wilson said and laughed. He climbed back into the truck, started it and took off, waving his hand.

Sam watched him go around the bend and then looked at the house.

It was a 1950s modern-style house with one floor in the front and two floors with a walkout basement in the back.

It was just as he remembered it, but it seemed smaller and more overgrown with vegetation. The small gingko tree in the front yard, which he had almost killed with an errant shotput toss when he was thirteen, was now over ten feet tall and flourishing. He hoped to be as resilient as that gingko tree.

He hesitated at the front of the yard. It was midday, and he realized that both of his parents were still at work. It wasn't even possible to tell them he was home since he didn't have their work phone numbers. He paced back and forth, dreading the upcoming meeting with his parents. Even knowing they were gone, he wasn't even sure he wanted to go in the house.

His trip had not been long, but he felt changed. The people he had met were different from him, and they were certainly different from each other. Everyone but Leonard was good and giving and willing to lend a hand when it was needed. He also felt more confident that whatever calamities might befall him, he would withstand them. Most, or perhaps all, of his issues would be worked out eventually. For now, he would live in the moment.

"What else could go wrong?" he said.

He was immediately sorry he had said it. He crossed his fingers and looked to the sky.

"I didn't mean that as a challenge, you know," Sam said out loud just to make it clear.

He sighed.

He would start looking for a job tomorrow. For now, he knew a way to jimmy a window in the back of the house. He decided to go in and call Cheryl.

32 ———————— December 1, 1969

Sam sat at his desk in the SAE fraternity house at Mizzou. His hair grew over his ears, and he was sporting a mustache. His roommate and a few friends were gathered in the room, including Mark Matthews. Sam had long since forgiven him for leaving him on a picnic table last spring, and now they told it to their friends as one of their many memorable drinking stories. But the mood was a lot more somber today than the one found with telling old stories. Instead, all were listening with bated breath to a man's voice on the radio. No one was speaking a word themselves.

Sam, his friends, and everyone else in the house were listening to the first airing of the draft lottery drawing, which had recently been introduced. All American men between the ages of eighteen and twenty-six were huddled near radios, waiting to hear their fates. It had to be one of the highest-rated broadcasts of all time.

A birthday date was being drawn for each of the 366 draft numbers. A low number was bad, and its owner would be the first to be drafted. Selective Service would start at the lowest available number and go to higher numbers as needed until the quota for each month was filled. No one really knew how high a number was safe. It was the first draft lottery drawing of the Vietnam War, so there was no history to go by. All that was really known was that Selective Service was now snapping men up at a rapid pace.

Draft deferments were still in effect. A 2S student deferment would still keep someone from being drafted, regardless of what his lottery number was. But if someone thought his number was high enough, he could volunteer to drop his deferment and become 1A, counting on his lottery number not coming up. If he remained 1A for a year without getting drafted, he then could only be drafted in a national emergency going forward. In the great game of draft tag, he would be home free. Sam knew that if he received a high enough number, he could stop worrying about the draft for good.

Static from the radio filled his dorm room and then subsided.

"Draft number nineteen," droned the announcer. "November 1."

"Fuck me!" screamed Mark Matthews.

He jumped up and threw a cup of pencils off the desk, showering half the room with pencil projectiles. He ran out the door, slamming it.

Mark still had his 2S deferment, but the lottery did not rescue him from the draft. He would always have that low number, and when he graduated and lost his deferment, he would be all the more vulnerable. Mark Matthews was far from home free in the game of draft tag.

When the lottery broadcast was over, Sam wandered the halls with his fraternity brothers, some downcast and some elated. All were drinking beer either in celebration or to deaden their despair. Mark was well underway and was adopting a what-the-hell attitude. Sam's number was 211, so he didn't know which line to stand in. The rate of men being drafted was not slowing down, and it was anyone's guess how high they would go. However, he still had his college deferment as a refuge. Even though that was not a permanent reprieve, he felt safer than he had felt in a long time.

Sam passed among his fraternity brothers, drinking beer and passing on congratulations or condolences.

Sam had experienced a challenging year. After coming home from the academy, he worked for a month at a roof truss factory near his house. He felt like he was a grunt again, only in civilian clothes. He felt lucky he was still in great shape, and he soon built up the skill to kill a fly with a hammer, although it was admittedly not the most marketable job skill. And he was bone tired at the end of each day. His job provided him with yet another reason, other than the draft, to stay in school.

Summer school classes at Mizzou started in late May. He enrolled in an insane number of classes, striving to reach the quota for his college deferment as soon as he could. Needing money, he worked at the Tiger Hotel in downtown Columbia. It was old and a bit faded, but still a grand hotel. Starting with parking cars, he moved up to delivering room service and eventually to working at the front desk. He even saved enough to manage to live at the SAE house with a few other summer-school students. Despite his misgivings about pledging in the fall, his good friends led to him eventually receiving the invite to join the fraternity.

But just as he was about to start classes, he received the letter. It told him in official language that he was 1A, only thirty-five days after he was discharged from the Air Force Academy. It was clear someone wanted his ass. The letter said he had thirty days to appeal.

He met with Major Robert Jennings, an army reserve major and head of the ROTC program at Mizzou, about his draft situation. To Sam's surprise, Major Jennings was sympathetic. He felt Sam's reclassification to 1A was suspiciously quick and agreed the chances of retaliation were real if he was drafted.

Jennings said, "I would not expect anything official, but you may get assigned to the most dangerous and nasty jobs by those gung-ho superiors who think you've squandered an opportunity they've been wishing for. Even if no one hurts or kills you, they could deny you the key support soldiers give one another. You could be ostracized, and that could be just as deadly."

He spent the rest of their time coaching Sam about delay tactics.

The first appeal was to the local draft board. Jennings told Sam to post the written appeal by registered mail on the deadline day. The local board took some time to process the appeal and then Sam had to appear before them. He stated his case. The elderly members of the board were not impressed, telling him so in a letter several weeks later.

His next appeal to the state draft board was in writing only. Again, he waited until the last minute to mail it. They took longer to deliberate before they turned him down. One last appeal to the national board remained. But before Sam mailed it, he was enrolled for the fall semester with an insane class load with enough hours to catch up. He appealed again to the local board. This time, when he received their reply, he had to read the letter three times before taking it in. He had won. It stated this would be pertinent on the condition that he successfully complete the courses. He was now only a few weeks from doing so. Check and double check. He had his college deferment back.

He had decided to accept his offer and pledge SAE in the fall. He didn't want to be a pledge, of course, but he loved the house and his fraternity brothers and thought they were both well worth going through it. At least as a sophomore, he got better treatment from the actives who were his own age. Many became close friends. Even during pledge harassment sessions, he was considered a pro by the actives because of his academy experiences. They knew they could not get under his skin, and he was largely left alone because of it.

He loved Mizzou. He was making great friends, and the atmosphere still felt like the same kind of magic he felt when he first arrived. There were always numerous opportunities for fun and adventure to be found as long as you looked for them in the right places. With the draft threat lessened in the fall semester, Sam was also getting a C− in saying no to all the good times around him.

For months, he and Cheryl had continued to write and call each other. But their lives, separated by distance, were beckoning them in different directions. No one asked to break up. They just called and wrote less. Then they did not call or write at all.

Epilogue ———————— October 1, 1976

Sam drove home in his lime-green Ford Maverick from work at KBDI, the public TV station in Denver. It was a Friday in 1976, and he was twenty-six years old. Gary Wright was singing "Love Is Alive" on the radio. The traffic was light, and his mind drifted to the events of the past years. Sam felt fortunate that he had survived the threatening buzzsaw of events that had led him to the present. He had attended the Missouri School of Journalism and graduated with a broadcast journalism degree. Then he loaded his Volkswagen Bug with all his possessions and moved to Denver.

Hordes of young people were enticed by the beauty and mystique of Colorado, but real jobs for them were rare. He found some temporary, menial construction work to pay the bills. He was getting accustomed to being the least useful end of the shovel as well as the low man on the construction crew totem pole. One foreman's highest goal each day was to make the college grad look stupid.

After moving on to sell vacation properties for a disreputable recreational real-estate company, which eventually went bankrupt, he found a job at a hunting and fishing magazine. Was this a real journalism job? Perhaps. On some days he felt more sure than others. He wrote the magazine's fishing forecast, which involved calling a few hundred lakes and fishing outfitters throughout the country. Sam learned a lot about fishing from his desk. There was much to absorb about the seasonal cycles of fish, which governed where they hung out, how they acted, and what they ate. He could soon sound like a pro and say things like, "They still hittin' the super doozies in the flats?"

It was also made clear that everyone had to sell some advertising to pull their weight. Sam thought that made sense, but it turned out that he had no talent for advertising sales. Eventually, he was fired for insufficient ad sales and a lack of what his editor called hutzpah.

He then landed a cameraman position at an educational TV station. He was working at what he loved during J-school. He particularly loved the camerawork in the field as well as using the big studio cameras with their Harley Davidson-like controls. Sam eventually rose to the position of producer/director. Although the pay was still not great compared to commercial TV jobs, the creative work was at least satisfying. He loved his work, made some good friends, and finally felt comfortable, secure, and best of all, included.

The draft rate decreased in 1970 and further decreased in 1971. Sam decided to revert to 1A status and rely solely on Selective Service not reaching his lottery number. They did not, so at last, he found himself home free. The word "lucky" did not begin to cover how he felt about missing Vietnam, and he was certainly thankful he did not have to go to Canada to do so.

Ho Chi Minh had led Vietnam since the 1940s, fighting the Japanese and the French before the US. At the time, he was still in charge. And after more than twenty-five years of fighting, what had been achieved? Sam could see how the US entered the war with good intentions, most believing they were helping the South Vietnamese against communist aggression. But in the end, the US struggled to disengage from the war, hoping that there was a way they could fix things in another fashion. TV images of the Vietnamese hanging from the last retreating American helicopters still burned in many minds.

His father had evolved from angry indifference to just indifference. Sam considered that a marked improvement. He often thought about whether he had made the right choice. If he had stayed another month instead of resigning, his grunt days would have been over. Life as an upper-class cadet would not have been so bad. He would likely be flying now. As it turned out, the Vietnam War had almost wound down by the time Sam would have graduated from the academy. In another year from now, he probably could have retired from the air force and become a commercial pilot. Perhaps it wouldn't have been such a bad life.

But then he thought about the cloistered lifestyle that would have continued to isolate him from the wider world. He had not been forced to kill or be killed. Instead, he had lived the new, vivid experiences of a free young man. And with that he could say that, yes, he had made the right choice.

Living at the academy had at least instilled in him a deep love of Colorado. Now just breathing the air gave him strength, and he felt a physical connection to the mountain towns, as if he had spent a past life as a gold miner there.

Sam arrived at his apartment. He unlocked his door and went in, heading into the kitchen and pulling a Coors beer from the refrigerator.

"Hi, honey," said Cheryl as she came around the corner from the hall, a wide smile on her face. She was wearing her work outfit: a blue skirt with a conservative white blouse. She had cut her auburn hair to midway down her neck. Sam sighed and felt himself relax from her smile. She walked to him, grabbed his head with both hands and planted a noisy kiss on his lips. Sam set down the beer and wrapped his arms around her. He buried his face in her hair and deeply breathed in her aroma. Their lips met.

Although he had dated others at Mizzou and in Denver, he had not been able to duplicate the intensity of his love for Cheryl. Beyond their passion was the trust and understanding from their deep friendship. She had taught him how to love . . . how to truly love. He thought of her often through the years.

He began thinking of her more after he moved to Colorado, living in the land where their love had blossomed. A year ago, he had begun searching phonebooks in the library for her name, hoping she was still there, in the same place she had also really loved. Not knowing which towns to search, he started where he had last seen her. When he saw her name in the Boulder phonebook, he was both excited and filled with trepidation. It had been years since they had last spoken, and he was sure she had found someone else. He waffled for several days before calling her.

When he did, Cheryl was both delighted to hear from him and amazed that he had ended up back in Colorado. She was teaching high school English in Boulder and was between relationships. She was eager to meet and suggested going to the Sink for old times' sake.

The next evening, Sam picked out the same outside table where they sat almost seven years ago. It was a beautiful spring night, rich with the smell of the blossoming air and the Sink's food. A full moon lit the sidewalk tables, where couples talked in low tones. He had bought flowers for the table. He wanted to be affectionate to Cheryl without seeming like a stalker. The very thought of her thinking anything like this was making his palms sweat. Was it too much? Would they even be able to start back up where they had last left off? He looked up and saw her coming toward him. Sam stood, did his best to push aside his anxiety, and held out his arms, daring to take a chance. In response, she moved to him quickly and hugged him tightly. They then kissed, albeit a little cautiously.

They ordered beer and pasta. As they ate, talked, and laughed, his worries melted away. This was Cheryl. What else had he expected? He felt like he had his best friend back.

It took several months to feel their way back to the romance they knew before. Sam was ready for romance immediately. But Cheryl said she needed to build the trust that he would not leave her again, even though she knew it was not his fault the first time. In the six months since, her misgivings had left her. They took turns staying at each other's place on weekends and travelled all over the mountains of Colorado—camping, hiking, and taking in the towns.

They had not untangled the logistics of fully living together. They both loved their jobs and coworkers, so Sam started making midweek sleepover trips to Boulder instead. That involved more than an hour to get there at the end of the day and another hour to commute back to his job in Denver the next morning, but it was worth it. It was only a matter of time before they would come up with a better solution. He was trying to get a job at the Boulder Educational TV station while she was checking out schools closer to Denver. It was not an overwhelming issue for either of them, and they both felt a lot more confident in both their love and their situation compared to what they were faced with seven years ago. They knew, for certain, they were going to live their lives together. They would figure it out. They owed each other that. Sam wished he would have learned this earlier, but he got there all the same. In the end, that's what mattered.

Cheryl and Sam were in his kitchen.

"How was your day?" she asked.

"Felt like the last day of school. I was just itching to come home and see you," he said, tucking a stray piece of hair behind her ear.

"Well, I'm here, and I'm all yours." She smiled.

Cheryl took a beer from the refrigerator and walked back over to Sam. She gently poked him in the ribs and said, "Take your shoes off, big boy. Come snuggle with me on the couch."

She danced across the living room and flopped backward onto the couch, adopting a fetching centerfold pose. Sam needed no further encouragement. He rushed over and lay beside her, burying his head in her breasts. She giggled as she held his head against her. Life was good.

Acknowledgments

I would like to offer thanks to numerous people who have significantly contributed to the writing and publishing of *Flightless Falcon*. This novel would not have been possible without the support, encouragement, and inspiration from the dedicated people that have touched my life along the way.

Brown Books Publishing Group guided me through the baffling waters of publishing my book and helped me improve it throughout the process. I thank Thomas Reale for deciding that *Flightless Falcon* was worthy of publication and for working with me in joining their team. I am grateful to my editors and proofreaders for their meticulous work in refining the manuscript. Their attention to detail and dedication to enhancing the language have elevated *Flightless Falcon* to new heights. Brittany Griffiths managed the project and kept me on track. As my developmental editor, Michael J. Totten taught me valuable lessons in writing fiction and suggested ways to reorganize the story's sections to unscramble my tangled timeline. Carissa Demma, who was my copy editor, ensured each sentence was correct and provided the greatest impact. Sterling Zuelch, who was my line by line editor, labored through every line of text to ensure every phrase and comma was "just so." Tom Ayars took the photograph for my author bio.

While writing the numerous revisions of *Flightless Falcon*, the following people endured my earliest efforts and provided useful feedback for multiple revisions. My thanks go out to Tricia Miller; Cindy Smith; Judy Kinard; my sister, Diane Faughn; and my daughter, Carrie Qualters. I want to give special thanks to Terry McKinnon, who also read my book several times and recommended it to Brown Books Publishing Group.

With profound gratitude and hope, I offer this book, hoping that it will touch the lives of those who read it as deeply as it has touched mine.

Music Playlist

In Order of Appearance

- "For What It's Worth" by Buffalo Springfield
- "Suzie Q" by Creedence Clearwater Revival
- "Hello, I Love You" by The Doors
- "People Are Strange" by The Doors
- "I Walk Alone" by Marty Robbins
- "Harper Valley PTA" by Jeannie C. Riley
- "My Way" by Frank Sinatra
- "This Guy's in Love With You" by Herb Albert & the Tijuana Brass
- "Wichita Lineman" by Glen Campbell
- "Aquarius" by The 5th Dimension
- "Ride My See-Saw" by The Moody Blues
- "The Old Rugged Cross" by George Bennard
- "Time of the Season" by The Zombies
- "I-Feel-Like-I'm-Fixin'-to-Die Rag" by Country Joe and the Fish
- "Satisfaction" by The Rolling Stones
- "In-a-Gadda-Da-Vida" by Iron Butterfly
- "It's Your Thing" by The Isley Brothers
- "Love Is Alive" by Gary Wright

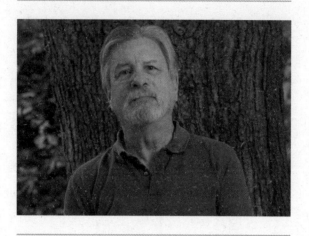

About the Author

James Charles Smith embarked on a journey from journalism to engineering before finding his true calling as a novelist. Born in Texas, he traveled widely as a US Air Force brat and then with his own wife and kids. He first attended college at the United States Air Force Academy and resigned during his first year, which is the inspiration for this story. He is a graduate of the Missouri School of Journalism from the University of Missouri. Following journalism school, he worked for various newspapers before settling down in television production. He worked for ten years as a writer, editor, cameraman, and producer/director, but it's a family tradition to change one's mind.

To better provide for his family, James returned to school for an engineering degree. As both an engineer and engineering manager, his duties included the writing and publishing of technical reports, engineering investigations, and training materials. Serving as a consultant to the Electric Power Research Institute, he edited their report on the instrumentation and control upgrade plan for the commercial nuclear power industry. Currently, he lives with his dog, Abel, in the foothills of Georgia's Blue Ridge Mountains. *Flightless Falcon* is his first novel.